GUILTY REFLECTIONS
REVISED EDITION

TERREL CARTER

iDream Publications

Note: This is a work of fiction. Names, places and incidents are products of the author's imagination or are used factiously. Any resemblance to actual events or locales or persons living or deceased, is entirely coincidental.
Published by: iDream Publications
P.O. Box 28910
Philadelphia, PA 19151
ISBN
Copyright: 2012
Guilty Reflections Revised Edition
Author Terrel Carter
Editing by Vern Robinson of V.R. Editing
Text Formation by Monique Ravenell
Cover design by LJ of Strickly Graphics

The sale of this book without its cover is unauthorized. If you purchased this book without a cover, you should be aware that it was reported to the publisher as unsold or destroyed. Neither the author nor the publisher has received payment for the sale of this stripped book.

PRINTED IN THE UNITED STATES OF AMERICA

Copyright 2012 Terrel Carter
All rights reserved, including the rights to reproduce this book or portions thereof in any form whatsoever.

ISBN-10: 0983596522
EAN-13: 9780983596523

Dedication

To My Main Man Speed,

I'm actually writing this dedication on the day of your funeral. Out of all the things I've ever written, this is one of the hardest. The tears won't stop coming as I reflect on our friendship and the fact that you were taken away from us too soon. I love you man and I will definitely miss you. We were kids growing up in a world that ate us alive. May God welcome you with open arms.

Acknowledgements

I would like to thank first and foremost my family: my beautiful wife Stacey, for her love and commitment to me, my mother Tonya, who inspires me to be so much more, my daughter Shante, my heart, my soul and my future. My grand baby Zya, Pop-Pop loves you. All my sisters, Li'za, Kim, Nafisah, Najibah, Kalima, Lachelle and Nikki. My brothers, Kurt, Muhammed, Masai, Ali, Pluck, Craig, and Damani (RIP). My father, Jamil, and my stepfather John, I pray God has embraced you both. I would also like to thank all my friends on the inside of these walls and outside of them who've remained steadfast in their friendships. Tashi, Rick, Dave, Dry, Dean Martin, Bap, Snag, Rip, Manchild, Shawna, Dawn, Gayle, Jody, Cook, Marlo, Rob Clark, Rob Miller, Booby, Kit, and Ari. There are so many people that have had an impact on my life on the outside of these walls that I know I've forgotten. If I have, forgive me and I promise, I got you on the next one. I would like to thank my homies that reside behind these forty-foot walls who know what it's like to lose the most precious thing a human being has – his freedom. Jamil, Lil Charlie, Jamo, Vern, Shadeed, Juan, Brick, Lou

Banks, Rob X, Muti, Kareem, Ghani, Yah Yah, Mu, Malik, Ali, Wavey, Black, Juice, Walt, Fannon, Slim, Wallo, Kev, and Gee. Last, but not least, all my nieces and nephews, Uncle Rell loves y'all. Oh yeah, I almost forgot, Lori, the first instructor I ever had that I actually like *(smile)*.

PROLOGUE

GUILTY REFLECTIONS
By Terrell Carter

"Going down both sides!" Rafique could hear the correctional officer's voice resonating up and down the prison block. It startled him a little as he lay on his bunk, caught in between a world of sleep and consciousness. This was his seventh day at Philadelphia's Detention Center and his body still hadn't adjusted to prison, so he slept through most of the day. Rafique jumped up and headed for the cell door before they threw the automatic lock. He needed to get to his friend's cell to get a pack of Newports. He was too late. A second before he grabbed the cell's door handle, he heard the lock click in place. *Shit, I only got a couple left. I hope we ain't locked down too long. I'd hate to be locked in this motherfucker with no cigarettes. Fuck, I need to quit.* Rafique took out a cigarette anyway and lit one up. He took a pull and blew the pale smoke into the air. His eyes followed the smoke as it drifted lazily towards the ceiling. He was use to being locked down for one reason or another because something was always going down in the county jail. Resigned to the facts of his circumstances, he took another drag off his cigarette and loudly exhaled it.

Fully awake and with nothing to do, Rafique walked back to his bunk, reached under his mattress, and retrieved the Donald Goines book he had been reading for the past couple of days. The story *Whoreson* had taken him out of the tiny cell he occupied and transported him back in time to the 1970's and the mean streets of Detroit, Michigan. Reading was a coping mechanism; it helped him take his mind off his own problems as he became absorbed into the life of a young black man's struggle to survive in a world of urban decadence.

Today, for some reason, his coping mechanism failed him. No matter how hard he tried, he couldn't get his mind to focus on the words in front of him. He gave up. Rafique laid the book on his lean chest and let his mind wander. He stared at the peeled paint on the ceiling. Ultimately, he knew where his mind would drop him off – 52nd and Delancey Street. The events that took place on that particular night would take him on the ride of his life, and in the end, lead him to the dimly-lit cell that he now occupied.

CHAPTER ONE

Traffic was thick and slow and the street lights were bright as the neighborhood hustlers, all ready to commence a night's work, took their post. Strutting back and forth under the spotlights of corner street lamps were all shapes and shades of chocolate eye candy, vying for the attention of the many young hustlers that populated the corners.

Fifty-Second Street, known by the residents of Philadelphia as "The Strip," was the pulse of West Philly. It was a nine block stretch of clothing shops, bars, delis and street vendors which sold everything from fitted baseball caps to bootleg tapes.

If you looked hard enough just below the surface of this consumer's paradise, you'd observe another life, the kind of life that wouldn't show up on a tour guide. Where young men decked out in their ghetto finest, cruised slowly up and down the four-lane street in the latest cars, blasting hip-hop music from their sound systems.

Congregations of young and old hustlers stood on the corners. Some had their very own clientele of crackheads and dope fiends, others didn't. All were busy scrambling, trying to realize a warped version of the American dream.

A crap game was in full swing on Delancey Street, one of the many small residential streets where most of the hustling took place. Rafique was participating in this crap game when Chisel-Head Mike pulled up in his money-green Acura Legend. Rakim's "Move The Crowd" was pumping loudly from Mike's Alpine sound system. The drum beat vibrated through Rafiques's body like a rhythmic heartbeat, causing his head to naturally move in time with the beat. Rafique backed out of the crap game counting a wad of bills. This day had been a good day. He smiled, revealing a small gap between his front teeth and called out to his friend Tashi, who like himself had just backed out of the crap game. "Yo, Tash, what time is it?"

"It's, uh, nine-thirty."

"Damn, it's still young out here. How many Dumb-Dumbs you got left?"

"Ummmm...I don't know, hold up." Tashi pulled out a small brown medicine bottle, opened it up, and began counting as he dumped some sky-blue pills into his hand. "I got twenty."

"Let me get ten of them jawns."

Tashi counted out ten of the pills and handed them to Rafique. Tashi watched as Rafique proceeded to take all ten of the pills. Rafique grimaced. The taste was a bad one. "Yo, let me get that Heineken. These motherfuckers are nasty." Rafique gagged but quickly fought back the gag reflex. To vomit now would be to waste a perfectly good high.

Rafique and his friends referred to the anti-anxiety pills Valium as "Dumb-Dumbs." If you took enough of them, like Rafique had just done, more than likely you would do something dumb and not remember any of it the next day. This is what happened to Rafique on this warm spring night. After taking the pills, Rafique's memory went from vague to blank.

Now as he lay on his flat, hard mattress, he racked his brain trying to recall memories that were as hard to capture as a shadow. *Goddamn!* His frustration was mounting, so he picked up the Donald Goines book and read a little more. It was fruitless. He couldn't focus on what he was reading. His mind wouldn't let him. Exasperated, he laid the book back on his chest and let his mind take him back again. This time his memory picked up right after his blackout and Fuzz had just been arrested for a homicide. He could remember hearing about Fuzz being arrested and he paid little attention to it, but after about a week, his name began to surface in connection with Fuzz and a murder.

At hearing the streets whispering his name, he was baffled, he began to worry. *How the fuck is my name all caught up with this nigga and a body? I don't even fuck with this dude like that. Them fucking pills. I hope I ain't do no dumb shit.*

As the chatter of his involvement grew louder, Rafique's instincts were screaming at him to leave town. But he ignored them. Not being totally foolish, he left the apartment that he shared with his woman, Tracey. As usual, his instincts were on point. Three weeks after Fuzz's arrest, he received a phone call from Tracey.

"Rafique, the police just left here and they said you killed somebody." Tracey's voice shook as she gripped the phone tightly. "Baby, they was asking me all these questions like did I know anything about it? I told them you ain't kill nobody, it was the other dude."

Tracey continued to talk, but Rafique could barely hear what she was saying. He was in a mild state of shock. *How the fuck did I get myself into this?*

"Rafique, baby, what are you going to do?" Tracey's question burned through the fog of shock, snapping him from his thoughts.

"Man, I don't know what the fuck I'ma do. Look...let me make a few calls. I'ma call you back in a few minutes."

"Okay, baby. Are you all right?"

"Yeah, I'm cool."

"I love you." Tracey's voice cracked as she struggled to hold back the tears before saying goodbye.

"I love you, too," Rafique responded before the dial tone was ringing in his ear. Rafique stared at the phone. The next call he had to make would be the hardest call he had made in his life. He began dialing his mother's number. He knew that the police would be to see her soon, kicking her door in looking for a suspected murderer. How do you tell your mother that you're wanted for a murder? Rafique paused in his dialing. He exhaled. He had to do it. Better the bad news came from him first than any other alternative.

Rafique shifted positions on his hard jailhouse mattress. He could still feel the pain in her heart and the shock in her voice when he told her what was going on.

✢ ✢ ✢

Early Sunday morning, Tonya, Rafique's mother, was at home relaxing. At the age of forty-three, she was the mother of five children, including Rafique and one stepson. With her two oldest children, Rafique and Kim, now adults, she had someone to watch over the little ones while she resumed her education. With two years of college under her belt, she was just beginning to take the steps needed to get her degree.

She had been married now for thirteen years and her marriage provided a stable home for Rafique and Kim. Before that, the children had to spend most of their time at their grandmother's home because of the long hours she had to put in on the job.

Tonya was a baby boomer and the oldest out of eleven children, so she was used to raising children. After Rafique was born, she moved out of her mother's home and into a small apartment in West Philadelphia. Three years after that Kim was born. The three of them stayed in West Philly for two more years before Tonya packed up and moved to Logan. It was then that she met and eventually married John. Once she was married, the family moved back to West Philly where John had a house. The family has been there ever since.

As a result of the marriage, Tonya had two more children, Masai and five years later, Kalima. Her children were close and with her stepson Damani coming over on the weekends, the household was filled with the laughter of children and plenty of love. Things would change though as the children got older.

Tonya worried about her oldest boy. Growing up, her son Rafique was a normal child, very quiet but extremely intelligent. He was the kind of child that things came easy for. He never had to study, but he still managed to ace all of his tests. His teachers used to tell her that he could be so much more if he would only apply himself. She tried everything to get him to comply, but it was useless.

Rafique's teenage years were when things took a turn for the worse. Initially, she was unaware of anything except for the fact that at times he could be disrespectful. Tonya figured that the disrespect was just an adolescent phase and her son was exerting his independence. Her perspective would change one day as she was straightening out his room. While going through his dresser drawers, she discovered a zip-lock bag full of marijuana; he was thirteen at the time. Things got progressively worse after that.

One night Tonya was awakened by the smell of smoke. Something was burning. Alarmed, she jerked her head off her pillow and looked at her digital alarm clock. It was 4:00 a.m. Carefully, she slid from under the covers and rose out of the bed. She didn't want to awake John. Tonya slipped on her robe and hurriedly made her way down the steps. The smell of smoke became stronger. It was coming from the kitchen. When she reached the kitchen, it was engulfed in smoke. She rushed to the stove to find an empty pot. All the water had evaporated – it was smoldering. She turned the fire off, opened the window, and immediately stared daggers at the person responsible, Rafique.

Rafique was sitting at the kitchen table asleep. His head was leaning against the kitchen wall, his mouth was open and drool was leaking agonizingly slow from his mouth. Tonya knew that look. She snapped, "Rafique!"

Rafique was startled out of his nod. "Huh?"

"What the hell is wrong with you? What are you on?"

Rafique could barely keep his eyes open and his voice was slurred. "I had some beer and weed."

"Don't no beer and weed have you nodding like a dope fiend! Are you drinking that syrup?"

"Naw, mom, I just had some beer and weed."

"Get on out of my kitchen and go on upstairs." Tonya's heart was broke. She knew that her son was drinking that codeine-laced cough syrup. She was losing her son to the same streets she had lost her younger brothers to. "Please Lord, save my son."

Maybe the God she prayed to wasn't the God of black boys because nothing she did, nothing John did, or nothing Rafique's father did could save Rafique from himself.

On top of all this, at sixteen Rafique had become a father. She shook her head as she recalled him bringing his fourteen-year-old girlfriend to the house. She tried to talk him out of having this baby, but Rafique wouldn't have it. He stated emphatically that he didn't believe in abortion. Tonya was shocked, and nothing she said or the parents of his girlfriend said could get their children to change their minds. Her son was making her a grandmother at the age of thirty-five. They were just children, too young for the kind of responsibility it took to raise a child.

Right after his daughter was born, Rafique was sent to reform school, which only made matters worse. By the time Rafique was eighteen, the streets had him like a fox caught in a steel trap. He was in and out of the county jails, and Tonya knew that it would only be a matter of time before he was either dead or in jail for a very long time. Tonya felt defeated. Her son, her firstborn, was becoming one of the grim statistics for young black men and she was powerless to stop it.

Finally, by the time Rafique was twenty-three, Tonya felt a little relief because her son had seemed to be slowing down. He had a job and he shared a nice apartment with his woman, Tracey. Tonya didn't care for Tracey too much because Tracey seemed a bit sneaky. But at the same time she seemed to be the reason why Rafique was slowing down. Things were looking up for Rafique and Tonya's mind was finally at ease.

This was the situation as Tonya lay in the bed watching a television evangelist swindle people out of their hard earned money. *That's a shame, $29.99 for a bottle of healing water.* The ringing of the phone interrupted her thoughts. She let it ring a couple times, hoping whoever was calling would hang up. No such luck. She picked up.

"Hello."

"Hey, mom."

"Rafique? It's a little early for you to be calling. What's wrong now?"

"Mom, I got some bad news."

Tonya gripped the phone tightly in anticipation of what Rafique would say next, as a slight pain in her temples began to take root.

"Mom, I don't how to say this."

"Rafique, whatever it is you have to say, just say it."

Tonya could hear Rafique's breath escape his mouth as he exhaled.

"Okay, mom, I'm wanted for a murder."

"What! What did you just say! What do you mean you're wanted for a murder?" One of her worse fears realized, her headache was in full bloom, pounding the sides of her head.

"Mom, this is the honest-to-God truth, I don't know what happened. I was high off some Valiums the night this happened. I can't remember if I was even there."

With her heart pounding in her chest and an intense pain throbbing in her temples, Tonya shook her head. "Rafique, baby, what have you gotten yourself into?"

CHAPTER TWO

"920053!"
Rafique was startled by the guard shouting out his number. Calling you by your number instead of your name is one of the many ways the state begins the process of dehumanization. Rafique looked towards the cell door. "Yo, man, what's up?'

"Pack your shit. You're going to the Burg," the guard said before quickly walking away.

The Burg, also known as Holmesburg, was a county jail that held prisoners with the most serious crimes that required the highest bails. This was the jail Rafique would be in while awaiting to go to trial. Rafique frowned and began to pack his meager belongings: a few pieces of mail, some books, soap, toothbrush, toothpaste, comb, brush, shampoo, and some underclothes. Item by item, Rafique dropped his belongings into a box while his mind was in overdrive. He desperately racked his brain trying to figure out how to defend himself against a murder charge when he couldn't remember if he was even involved.

Riding on the Blue Goose prison bus, handcuffed and shackled in pairs, Rafique and about twenty other young

Black and Hispanic men, deep in their own thoughts, took the trip to Holmesburg.

The old prison bus rattled violently and hit a pothole. This caused their cuffs to tighten up, squeezing bone and causing shouts of anger and pain to fill the bus. Rafique, with his face balled up in discomfort, stared out the window. Women waved as the Blue Goose lumbered past as if the men were off to war, seemingly never to return. He paid them no mind, his thoughts preoccupied with Philadelphia's most notorious jail, The Terror Dome. It was nicknamed rightly so, after Public Enemy's song "Welcome To The Terror Dome."

Arriving at the prison after a ten minute ride, they were driven through the Sally Port. The Sally Port was more or less a drive-thru auto garage with a dry grease pit where a guard did a thorough underbelly search of the vehicle. After that was done, the bus slowly pulled up to the reception area where the prisoners were unloaded two pair at a time and herded into the reception area. As the corrections officer took the handcuffs and shackles off, Rafique looked around at his new surroundings. *This joint looks like a fucking dog kennel and it stinks in this motherfucker.* It was a putrid smell, the kind of smell that seeped through your pores and stayed with you for hours. It was an odor that was a mix of stagnant piss, vomit, muslim oil, and watered-down disinfectant. It permeated throughout the entire room via body heat and a neglected ventilation system.

"920053 Rafique Johnson!"

Rafique looked up at hearing his name called and then navigated his way through the crowd of prisoners to the front of the room where the guard stood.

"You 920053?" the guard asked.

"Yeah."

"Step over here please."

Rafique walked over to the next empty cell that the guard pointed at and waited.

"Okay, now strip."

Each time Rafique was ordered to do this emasculating act, the humiliation felt brand new. He stared at the guard before slowly complying. Was that a spark of lust in the guard's eyes? It may have been. Some guards actually enjoyed staring at other men's nakedness.

Oblivious to Rafiques's hard stare, the guard continued. "Let me see your hands. Open your mouth, stick out your tongue, run your fingers through your hair, lift your balls up. Turn around lift up your left foot, your right foot. Okay now, bend over and spread 'em."

The coup de grace – "bend over and spread 'em." This was where the humiliation reached its peak. Rafique couldn't help but to think of and identify with the first Africans that were kidnapped and brought to this foreign land. He shared their shame and humiliation as they were forced upon auction blocks while groups of white men sized them up for purchase. He felt the pain and the feelings of helplessness as if his ancestors reached out from centuries past and exposed Rafique to an abuse that time had seemed to forget.

After the humiliating ass-crack search was over, he was issued the basic necessities, which consisted of a light-blue shirt, dark blue pants, and some sheets wrapped up in a towel. After about two hours, all the prisoners were processed and escorted down Soup Alley. Soup Alley was a corridor that led to the cell-blocks. As they made their way down Soup Alley, they walked past the chow hall and a menagerie of feral cats, big black rats, and flying cockroaches.

A seasoned prisoner hollered out, "Welcome to the Terror Dome!"

All heads turned in search of the author of the voice, but no one was in sight as they continued to the end of Soup Alley. Once out of the corridor they came upon the "Center." It was just as the name implies, the center of operations.

Holmesburg Prison was designed after the first U.S. prison, Eastern State Penitentiary. Both of their designs were based off the Octupi Premise; the cell blocks made up the tentacles of the octopus, and its brain was, as is in the case of the prison, its center of operations.

When Rafique first laid eyes on the center, he couldn't help but to think of a board game he used play as a child – Trouble. The prison was set up exactly like the game board. Walking past center, the group of new prisoners stopped at each block where the guard assigned them to their block. Rafique was dropped off on J-block.

When Rafique entered the block the first thing he noticed was the size. It was almost equivalent to a city block in length. Rafique stood at the entrance. He gazed at the cells running down a narrow corridor all the way to the back through a river of miserable and frustrated faces. The guard told him he was assigned to cell 1092 all the way in the back. Eyes forward, Rafique began to walk through that river of misery.

There were about one hundred and fifty men standing around talking. Some of the guys had dragged their bed frames out of their cells and were playing cards or other board games on them. As Rafique continued towards the cell, he didn't see one familiar face, which was a first for him. Whenever he came to jail, people he knew would always be there. The same people who he ran with on the streets were the same people who populated the jails.

Rafique arrived at the cell and almost slipped from the water that flooded the floor, which came from the leaky pipes that ran at the top of cells all the way down the length of the block. The doors to the cells were flat metal bars criss-crossing one another, leaving small squares in the middle that were used to pass food trays through in case the jail was locked down. Rafique stepped into the cell and noticed that the cell was as wide as, and at least half the length of a subway car. There were two beds across from one another that were wedged against the walls. The ceiling was at least ten feet high with a skylight stuffed with dirty towels. On the right-hand side of the entrance was a dirty sink that was connected to a dirty toilet. In the back of the cell was a small rectangular window with bars and a filthy screen. The cell was also occupied by a young Puerto Rican man who was sitting on one of the beds.

"What's up? I'm Rafique, the guard sent me down here. I'm your new celly."

"Que pasa, what's up? I'm Angel," he responded as he extended his right hand. Rafique shook the offered hand before sliding his box under the empty bunk and sitting down on the cardboard-thin mattress.

The new cellies talked for the next couple hours, getting to know one another. Rafique learned that Angel was a laid-back type of guy from the Badlands of North Philly, who like himself, was awaiting trial on a homicide.

After they finished talking, Rafique began making up his bed. *This is alright with me. Angel doesn't talk much, plus I don't feel like being around no talkative motherfucker no way.*

After his bed was made, Rafique kicked off his black Bo Jacksons, took his blues off, and placed them along with a couple of books under his mattress to prop it up. He needed a makeshift pillow. Rafique lay down and almost immediately his mind went back to when he went on the run and how paranoid and desperate he felt.

CHAPTER THREE

WASHINGTON, DC
JULY 6, 1991, 8:00PM

The lonely wail of the police siren snatched the extremely paranoid Rafique out of a dream and back into reality. His mind, still fighting off the last vestiges of sleep, instinctively moved his tired limbs into action. He jumped up from the twin bed and stumbled blindly to the window. Slowly Rafique pulled back the drawn curtains. The light from outside parted the sea of blackness that shrouded his motel room. Furtively, Rafique's eyes darted back and forth. Up and down the streets they searched. *There go that motherfucker right there.* His eyes barely able to focus, Rafique zeroed in on the lone police cruiser that sped past, lights flashing and sirens screaming. The thundering of his heart began to subside as relief washed over him. Rafique walked back to his bed and lay down.

He had been in DC a little over a month now, holed up at the Walter Reed, a seedy motel right off Georgia Avenue in the Northwest section of the city. Because he had family in DC, it was the first place he thought of when the police came looking for him. He'd been to DC numerous times over the years visiting family and friends, and because of that fact, he was no stranger to the Capital. Rafique knew how to get around and how to get some money, which he desperately needed. He was on the verge of being broke.

Fully awake now, Rafique slipped on some sweatpants, a tee shirt, and some Nike flip-flops. He then left out the motel room to use the phone right outside his room's door. Rafique dropped a quarter into the pay phone and called his step-brother Pluck. Pluck was the son of his father's wife, Lorraine. He stood about five-foot-ten and was slightly overweight. At eighteen, he had just graduated high school and was stuck where a lot of teenagers get stuck, not really knowing what direction to take in life. Pluck was a little naïve to the streets but a quick thinker and trustworthy. Rafique trusted Pluck, and because of that trust, Rafique knew he could depend on him.

"Hello," Pluck answered after one ring.

"Pluck, what's up? It's me, Rafique."

"What's up, Rafique?"

"I'm on my way up there. Meet me at Fort Totten, I'm a little fucked up right now and I need to get me some paper."

"What time you gonna be up here?"

"I'll be up there like in like two hours."

"Alright, youngin, I'ma see you when you get here."

Rafique hung up the phone and went back inside to get dressed. Living out of a couple Nike duffle bags, he pulled out a black and red Fila sweatsuit and laid it on the bed before taking a quick shower. After showering, he dried off, put on some silk boxers, and sprayed on a little Drakar cologne. Rafique wiped the steam off the bathroom mirror, brushed his teeth and smiled at his reflection, revealing a small gap and a chipped right tooth. Brushing his hair, Rafique began to think of when he was child and how he hated being dark skinned. He could recall clearly all the names the other children used to call him: blackey, midnight, tarbaby, buckwheat, black ass. *Damn, they used to give me the blues. I wonder if white kids grow up hating to be white.* As these thoughts raced through his mind, he smiled again at his reflection. Rafique liked the image that smiled back. He stood at an even five-foot-eight and weighed in at a slight one hundred and forty pounds. With thick, short cut, wavy hair and small slanted eyes, he had grown, despite the negative imagery, to like how he looked. Although he still suffered from a slight complex about his skin tone, he had come miles away from where he was as a child.

By the time he had exited the bathroom, Rafique was in a hurry. He headed to the bed and subsequently stubbed his toe against the nightstand, "Fuck!" He shouted out in pain and anger while hopping around on one foot. After the pain subsided, Rafique limped over to the nightstand and picked up the lamp that had fallen. It wasn't broken, but the bulb had blown out. Rafique sat the lamp back up and made a mental note to get some more bulbs while he was out.

Rafique slipped on his sweat suit and red Fila T-shirt. He then reached over, picked up his pillow, retrieved his black 9mm, and tucked the shiny gun in his waistline and pulled the drawstring tight. After that, Rafique put on his Air Force Ones and stepped out into the fading sunshine.

The air was thick, almost suffocating. Sweat beads immediately formed on his brow. *It's hot as shit out here.* Rafique removed his jacket and headed the one block away to Alaska Avenue where his black, 1990 Honda Accord was parked. Rafique heard a car slowly approaching from behind. He took a quick glance in that direction. Was that the police? He was shook. The paranoia that was a constant companion had him seeing and hearing things that weren't really there. *Just a regular car with regular people in it. I need me some fucking Dumb-Dumbs. Listen to you, you idiot. That's the shit that got you all fucked up now.*

Rafique reached his car and pressed the alarm button on his key ring, disengaging the alarm. Once inside his car, he pulled out his Brand Nubian tape, popped it in the tape deck, turned the car on, and pulled off as the hit song "Slow Down" exploded from the sound system.

By the time he was pulling into North Capital Street into the parking lot of Fort Totten, the sun had completely set. Street lights lit up the nighttime skies with an artificial glow, allowing Rafique to find a parking spot. He parked, got out the car, and headed up the walkway towards the apartment buildings.

Fort Totten is an apartment complex in the Northwest section of the city. A lot of hustling took place in Fort Totten, and as Rafique made his way towards the three buildings it wasn't surprising to see crackheads speeding back and forth in search of someone to feed their addiction.

"Ay, youngin, you doing something?" Rafique was asked by a grimy-looking crackhead as he continued to walk towards the buildings.

"Yeah, give me like ten...fifteen minutes, though."

"Alright, youngin."

Rafique continued on. He was a little surprised that there was no one outside selling coke. *What the fuck is going on? Where the fuck is everybody at? Man, I hope the police ain't been up here.* There was always someone outside selling coke, so for there to be no one around was strange.

Rafique arrived at the middle building and stopped to enter. At the same time, the door opened up and Pluck walked out. "Yo, Fique, what's up, youngin?"

"What's up, Pluck?"

The brothers embraced and shook hands. "Fique, ain't nobody out here tonight. They all went to the Underground, so you should be able to get some paper quick. Look at all these smoking-ass bamas out here. Black Rob is upstairs. He got some fifties. I told him you was on your way out here and you would probably want to holla at him."

Rafique dug into his pocket and pulled out his last two hundred dollars and handed it to Pluck. Pluck took the money, turned around, and walked into the building with Rafique right behind him. On the way up the steps, Rafique stopped on the first floor. "Yo, you don't need me up there with you. I'ma be in the house with Eesh."

"Alright, I'll be right back."

Pluck headed one flight up and Rafique pulled out a key to Aisha's front door.

Aisha was nineteen and about as close to perfect as you could get. All the young men from Fort Totten hung out and hustled in front of the building she lived in. This was where Rafique first met her two years ago when Pluck first brought him around.

He noticed her immediately. Her honey-brown complexion glistened with sweat on that hot summer night. She was fine, sitting in a beach chair, listening to a walkman. Rafique noticed her staring, but he played it off like he didn't. There were two reasons he refused to hold her stare. The first being she was too fine not to be involved with one of the many young men who were hanging out. Rafique was a new face and he didn't want to step on anyone's toes. The second reason was something his uncle Wease told him a long time ago: "*Rafique, women, especially fine women who are confident, are used to men coming at 'em all the time. So when they come across a man they're attracted to and he acts as if she doesn't exist, that will sometimes make the attraction stronger. Now she's trying to figure you out, wondering what's up with you, and why you ain't coming at 'em. At that point it's a challenge, a challenge to obtain that which they think they can't have.*"

Recalling these words of wisdom, Rafique kept up the act. He continued to ignore her. He wouldn't respond when she stared or smiled at him. He didn't keep the charade up for long, though. How could he? She was too fine to ignore for long.

After a few days he gradually started showing a little interest. Little by little they became closer. Once he got to know her, she opened up to him and revealed that she had a thing for him from the very first time she laid her eyes on him. Rafique was amused when she recalled how he used to ignore her subtle, sometimes bold, advances and how his strategy made her want him even more. Up to this point, everytime Rafique laid eyes on Aisha he silently thanked his uncle for his advice. Because without it Rafique would have been lumped in the same category as a lot of other guys—which had the potential, she revealed, to get boring real fast. All these thoughts raced through Rafique's mind as he turned the key to her front door.

✫ ✫ ✫

Aisha sat in her two-bedroom apartment alone. At nineteen years old, she lived by herself. Her mother had been gone for two years and moved in with her boyfriend, leaving Aisha the apartment. Aisha's mother felt secure leaving Aisha on her own. She also still kept a key and she would stop by everyday when she first left, to make sure Aisha was doing okay. As time went on, her visits grew less frequent. It was as if she slowly weaned her daughter of her presence.

Aisha clicked the remote to the television. *All these damn channels and ain't shit on TV. I'm ready to get this cable shit turned off.* Aisha turned off the TV, walked to the bedroom, and put on her Guy tape. Aaron Hall's baritone voice soothingly flowed from the speakers.

> BABY, YOU CAN HAVE ALL OF ME,
> BUT I'M NOT TOTALLY FREE,
> I WISH THIS COULD LAST,
> FOREVVVEEERRRR...

"I love this song," Aisha said to herself. It reminded her of the first time she laid eyes on Rafique. His brother Pluck had brought him around one day about two years ago. She had been sitting in her beach chair in front of her building on that hot summer night. She had her walkman on and was listening to the same song she was listening to now, "Piece Of My Love," when Pluck and his brother walked up. She turned the volume down as Pluck was introducing him to the guys from the neighborhood. *Rafique, huh? He probably one of them mooslims.* Then she heard him speak. *He got an accent, too. He probably from upstate somewhere, with his chocolate self.* Aisha boldly stared at Rafique, hoping he would respond to her obvious flirting.

When he didn't, she loudly sucked her teeth, rolled her eyes, got up, and stormed into the house.

Weeks went by before he even spoke to her. So when he finally stepped to her, she was hooked. Getting to know him, she learned that he was from Philly, he was twenty-one, and he was in town visiting family for the summer. They became very close over those summer months. So much so, that when he went back to Philly, he returned every other week just to be with her.

Things continued in this manner for a couple years, and although she needed to be with him more, she never complained because she believed that one day soon he would came to visit and never leave.

One day about a month ago Aisha got a call from him. "Eesh, I'm in town. I'm staying at the Walter Reed. I'ma be in town for a while, but I'll be staying here. You got some money?"

"Yeah, baby, I got some."

"Alright, order me a pizza. I'ma be over there in a minute."

Aisha was so happy at the time that she didn't think to ask him why he was staying at that motel or why he didn't call her before popping back in town. All she could think of was her man was back and he was on his way.

Those questions she didn't ask then were her thoughts now as she lay on her back listening to her tape. Just then, her thoughts were interrupted by her front door opening and closing. *I hope that's Rafique.* Aisha quickly got up and walked into the living room.

"Hey, baby." Aisha's smile lit up the apartment. It was Rafique who had entered her home.

Rafique returned her smile with one of his own. He was just as happy to see her as she was to see him and her words dipped in a slow southern drawl, were music to his ears as he walked towards her.

Aisha threw something extra into her walk. She bit her bottom lip, squinted her already slanted eyes, and seemingly floated across the room towards him. They closed the distance between them, embraced, and kissed passionately.

Damn, this a fine motherfucker. Her body felt as soft as a feather bed pressed up against him. Reluctantly he released her. His eyes followed the sway of her hips as she strutted towards the couch and took a seat. At five-foot-five and one hundred and twenty-five pounds, in his eyes her body was perfect. She had a small waist that opened up into some curvaceous hips that supported two basketball-like ass cheeks. Her breasts were in perfect proportion with the rest of her body, about the size of two apples, kind of small, but a little bit more that mouthful. On this particular day she had a pair of skin-tight shorts and a cut-off shirt that showed her flat belly. Rafique took a seat opposite her on the black leather sofa, reached in his pocket and pulled out his cigarettes. Aisha squinted at him as he lit his Newport.

"What you looking at?" Rafique asked, blowing smoke rings in the air.

Aisha smiled, displaying a deep set of dimples. She got up and headed to the kitchen. Rafique watched as she reached on top of the refrigerator and grabbed a bag of chips. Rafique smiled as her shirt rose and exposed the lower portion of her breast. She wasn't wearing a bra.

"Rafique, you want something to drink?"

"Naw, Eesh, I'm cool."

Aisha returned to the living room munching on the chips and took a seat on his lap. "Are you gonna spend some time with me today, baby?" Aisha asked while feeding Rafique some chips.

Rafique chewed up the chips and sucked the salt off her fingers. "Yeah. But right now, I got something I need to do. I'm fucked up right now, Eesh, I need to get me some money."

Before she could respond, there was a knock on the door.

"Eesh, go answer that, it's probably Pluck."

Aisha pouted but she got up. Rafique was right. Pluck walked into the apartment and headed straight for him. "Yo, I got that," Pluck said, handing Rafique four fifties. Pluck sat down facing Rafique and began eagerly rubbing his hands together.

Rafique took the cocaine and laid it out on the glass coffee table that was located in between the sofa and matching love seat. The small cut up pieces of cocaine resembled white pieces of soap. Rafique marveled at how something so insignificant-looking could cause a pleasure so intense that it could be chased forever, leaving nothing but misery, death, and incarceration in its wake.

"Eesh, hand me that razor on top of the TV," Rafique said, turning towards her.

Aisha put her remote down, got up, grabbed the razor, and handed it to Rafique. She then sat back down next to him, picked the remote back up, pulled her knees to her chest, and continued to watch TV.

Razor in hand, Rafique began chopping up the fifties, breaking them down to twenties. Out of one fifty you get five twenties, doubling whatever you spend. Without looking up, Rafique addressed Pluck. "Look, man, I'ma go outside. Stay in here by the window so when I start running low I can holla up to you. You can bring me some more coke down, then come back in wait for me to call you again."

Moments later, Rafique finished chopping up the fifties. He grabbed a few of the twenties and headed out the door.

The crackheads had been waiting for hours for someone to show up with some coke, so as soon as Rafique stepped outside they were on him like a Black Friday shopper chasing a 50% off sale. He was surrounded by hands tightly gripping money and what seemed like a thousand voices demanding to be served.

"Hold the fuck up! Back up! Give me some motherfucking room! As a matter of fact, line the fuck up! I ain't selling shit until you motherfuckers get in line!"

Rafique was like the pied piper leading the rats out to sea as the crackheads got in line. Once some semblance of order was established, things moved fast. In a matter of seconds he was calling up to Pluck. Things were moving so fast, it seemed like in a blink of an eye it was four in the morning. Rafique checked his watch. *Man, fuck all this, I'm done.* By this time the human traffic had slowed to a crawl. After coming in a steady stream, the crackheads had started to come in waves. Initially, the waves came every five minutes or so, but now they came like every half hour or forty-five minutes. Rafique served the last of them and waited around for a few minutes—in case of stragglers—and then he headed back inside.

Pluck was still up watching TV, but Aisha had retired to her bedroom, which was a good thing for Rafique. Aisha had a tendency to get on his nerves about staying out late. Rafique yawned. The long night was starting to catch up to him. He walked over to the coffee table and began pulling out his money. It was everywhere, in his pants pockets, jacket pockets, and even in his socks. He started counting, $3500.00 after coming outside with two hundred. The day couldn't have turned out better.

"Damn, Rafique, you need to go ahead and get a couple ounces." Pluck was always trying to get Rafique to reinvest his money in more cocaine.

Rafique ignored him. He really didn't like selling coke. He hated what it did to people. He experienced firsthand the devastating effects of this drug and how it turned some real good people into some down-and-out fiends.

One of his aunts, a hard-working woman who liked to have her weekend card games, was introduced to the drug and it nearly destroyed her life. Rafique witnessed his aunt's slow decline from a hard-working woman to a desperate fiend. He watched as she struggled to break the iron grip the drug had on her.

He would often get into disputes, sometime physical, trying to persuade people not to sell his aunt drugs. It was at that point he realized he was being hypocritical by telling people not to sell drugs to his aunt but at the same time selling it to other peoples' family members. But now he was a fugitive, on the run for a murder, and he needed cash. And just like the old cliché "desperate times call for desperate measures," Rafique put his morals to the side and did what he felt he had to do.

After Rafique finished counting the money, he peeled off five hundred and gave it to Pluck. "Yo, I'm going to bed. You staying over?"

"What you think? It's late as shit. I ain't going nowhere."

"Alright, I'ma see you in the morning." Rafique left Pluck in the living room and proceeded to the bedroom. Aisha was sleeping peacefully when he entered the bedroom. He tiptoed over to the bed and gently placed a kiss on her forehead.

Aisha woke up with an attitude. "Damn, Rafique, what about my time? You were out there all night."

Rafique's face betrayed his irritation. "Look, Eesh, if you want to start this kind of shit, I can leave. I really ain't trying to hear no nut shit. I've been out there dealing with them crazy motherfuckers all night. The last thing I need right now is to listen to some fucking nagging"

Aisha bit her bottom lip, fighting back a sarcastic reply. "Are you staying over or what?"

"Yeah, peanut head, I ain't going nowhere."

"Could you give me a minute, baby? I need to go to the bathroom and freshen up."

"Yeah, but don't be all long, I might fall asleep."

"That's alright, I know how to get you up."

Rafique smiled as Aisha got up and left the room. He knew what was next, so he began to prepare. The first thing that he did was light the scented candles that were already placed strategically around the bedroom. The room immediately began to fill with the scent of jasmine. Rafique loved this scent. He took a deep whiff before turning on the stereo system. A quick search of the tapes that lined the top of the dresser turned up his slow-jam mix-tape.

Rafique picked the tape up, inserted it into the tape deck, and pushed play.

  SLOOOOWWWWLLLLYYY MY EEEYYYEEESSS
     BEGAN TO SEE,
    THAT I NEED YOU HERE,
  RIGHT WITH ME AT ALL TTTIIMMMEESS…

The room filled with the soulful harmonies of Boyz II Men as Rafique began to undress. Stripped down to his boxers, Rafique stood at the foot of the bed looking over the bedroom, making sure everything was just right. He didn't notice Aisha until he felt her arms envelop him in a soft caress. Rafique spun in her arms to face her. No words were necessary as he placed a wet kiss on her forehead. She moaned. His lips sent electric chills racing up and down her spine. Gently he picked her up and placed her on the bed. Her eyes were glazed with passion as she watched him remove his silk boxers. He climbed onto the bed, his eyes never leaving hers. He kissed her feet and traveled the length of her body, leaving a wet trail in his wake. Their bodies became entwined in a physical manifestation of true love as Renee and Angela's "You Don't Have to Cry" covered them like a crushed velvet comforter on a harsh winter night.

An hour later, Aisha rolled off him and laid her head on his chest. "Rafique, I love you so much."

"I love you, too, baby."

They lay there like that breathing heavily until sleep, like a professional kidnapper, came out of hiding and took them hostage.

Rays of sunlight sliced through the curtain cracks in the bedroom, allowing streaks of light to cut through darkness. It was early afternoon and Rafique, who had just awakened, smacked his mouth open and closed as the unsavory taste of morning breath wreaked havoc in his mouth.

Rafique reached over to the nightstand next to the bed and turned on the lamp, flooding the room in light. He swung his legs over the side of the bed, sat up, and yawned before getting up and heading to the bathroom. Just before he reached the door he stopped, turned around, and looked at Aisha as she slept. *That's my baby, but I miss the shit out of Tracey. They so different, but it's like whatever one don't have, the other one do. I love them both for different reasons and if I had to choose, I don't think I could.* Rafique shook his head and quietly walked back to the bed. He stared a moment longer before kissing her gently on the cheek. Without a sound, he turned and walked to the bathroom.

After washing up, he re-entered the bedroom, slipped on his clothes, and walked out to the living room. Pluck was still asleep, snoring lightly. *I can't believe this motherfucker still a virgin. Before the day is out I'ma change all that.* "Yo, Pluck! Get up, man! It's time to go!"

"Alright, youngin, give me like five more minutes," Pluck answered, still half asleep.

Rafique walked over to the sofa and snatched the sheet off Pluck. That woke him up completely.

"Damn, youngin, what the fuck you do that for?"

"Yo, come on, man, before you wake up Eesh and she come in here bitching about me leaving."

Pluck reluctantly got up and headed to the bathroom. Thirty minutes later they were back at Rafique's motel room. Rafique jumped straight into the shower, washed up, and got dressed. "Yo, I be right back." Rafique addressed Pluck, heading towards the front door, "I got to go to the pay phone."

Pluck nodded his head.

Rafique stepped outside. The cloud-filled skies produced a mugginess that instantly made Rafique perspire. "Damn, it's hot out this motherfucker," Rafique mumbled to himself as he wiped the sweat from his brow. Arriving at the phone booth, Rafique picked the receiver up and began dialing numbers. First, a calling-card number to pay for the call, and then the ten-digit number to his apartment in Philly. He missed Tracey and had been neglecting to call her, and right now he needed to hear her voice. The phone rang a few times before a woman's voice spoke through the receiver. "Hello."

CHAPTER FOUR

The apartment felt empty as Tracey sat in her love seat. She was home alone, just getting in from dropping Tim-Tim off at his grandmother's house. The emptiness she felt was worsened by the gray skies outside that cast a bleak mood over the apartment.

Tracey got up, walked over to her entertainment system, and popped in her Jodeci tape. She turned the volume up and "Forever My Lady" filled the apartment with Joe-Joe's soulful second tenor.

> SO YOUR HAVING MY BABY,
> AND IT MEANS SO MUCH TO MEEEE.
> THERE'S NOTHING MORE PRECIOUS,
> THAN TO RAISE A FAMILY...

Tracey walked back over to her love seat and sat down. The empty feeling that was infecting her entire being wasn't just because of the loneliness or the depressing weather outside; it was also because the man she loved had left her. Tracey closed her eyes and began to think of the man she loved and how much she missed him. With a picture of his face floating in her mind's eye, she let Kay-Cee and Joe-Joe's smooth lyrics take her on a trip down memory lane. She went back to when she was a teenager and the day she had met Rafique. She could recall that moment clearly as if it had just occurred yesterday.

On this particular day, Tracey had stayed over her girlfriend Wanda's house for the weekend. They were up playing on the phone when Wanda suggested that they call Rafique. Tracey knew who Rafique was, but she didn't know him personally.

"Tracey, you got to call him. He knows my voice," Wanda said, handing Tracey the phone as she dialed Rafique's number. Tracey grabbed the phone and put the receiver to her ear just as a male voice came over the line. "Hello."

"Hello, can I speak to Rafique?"

"Speaking. Who this?"

"It's Rhonda." Tracey gave a fake name and swallowed her chuckle.

"Rhonda? Rhonda who?"

"I got your number from my girlfriend. I've been wanting to talk to you for a while now. I go to West Catholic. I be seeing you all the time on 46th Street."

"Oh yeah? What you look like?"

"I'm, uh, brown skin, five-six…I got thick eyebrows and I be wearing Laura Beggati's all the time."

"Oh yyeeaahhh. I know who you are. I be seeing you on 56th Street a lot."

"Yeah, I live on 56th Street."

"You know what? I've been wanting to talk to you, too. I just never had the opportunity."

Suddenly, Tracey broke off the conversation. "Huh? Uh, Rafique, my mom wants to use the phone. I'ma have to call you back."

"Damn, hold up, ain't you gonna give me your number?"

"Not right now. I'll give it to you when I call back." Tracey hung up the phone and she and Wanda got a good laugh at Rafique's expense.

A few days later she was standing on the El train's platform when she heard someone call out from behind her.

"Ay! Rhonda!"

Tracey turned around in the direction she heard the voice and stared straight into Rafique's eyes.

"Hey, Rafique. Look, my name ain't Rhonda. Me and Wanda was playing on the phone that night. My real name is Tracey. I really wanted to meet you, that's why I gave you a real description of myself."

After that encounter they exchanged numbers and began calling each other. At the time this was as far as the relationship would get. Tracey had a man at the time that she was crazy about, so talking on the phone was the farthest she would take it. Rafique could sense that she wasn't willing to take the relationship any further, so he moved on, but they remained friends.

A few years had passed since that time, and Tracey had grown into a young woman. She was twenty-three and a single mother when Rafique popped back into her life. She remembered that day just as clear. She had just gotten out of the shower when she heard the doorbell. Tracey was hoping it was her son's father as she quickly wrapped a towel around herself and walked to the door.

"Who is it?"

"It's Rafique. Is Tracey home?"

Tracey opened the door and smiled. She hadn't seen or heard from Rafique in a long while. "Hey, stranger, long time no see."

"What's up, girl? I see you just got out the tub."

Tracey realized that all she had on was a towel and she began to blush. "Yeah, I thought you was my son's father bringing my son home."

"Are you disappointed it's not?"

"No. Plus, I don't fuck with him no more like that anyway."

"Well, I was dropping by to see how you was doing. I tried calling you but your number was disconnected."

"Yeah, we got a new number."

"Yeah, well that's why I'm here now. I just came back from out of town and I wanted to see you. Look, I'ma let you go ahead and get dressed. Plus, I got somewhere I need to be. So let me get your number so I can call you. You know, maybe we can get together sometime, go out or something."

Tracey gave Rafique her number and that was the beginning of their relationship. In the beginning, they spent a lot of time together, getting to know one another. Before long they became very close. Her son really took a liking to him, and that was a plus because she couldn't have a man in her life without considering the impact it would have on her boy. After months of being together, they made their relationship official by moving in together.

The Jodeci tape came to an end, bringing Tracey out of her memories. She rubbed her stomach and thought of the new life that was forming in her womb. Tracey was confused though. Rafique was gone – a fugitive on the run for a homicide. She missed him terribly, but at the same time, she was angry. *How could he do this to me? Leave me alone with a son and another baby on the way. Why hasn't he called? He's been gone now for three weeks. Fuck this, I need to start thinking about myself now. I can't afford to be relying on him no more.* Just then, Tracey's thoughts were interrupted by the phone. She picked up on the first ring. "Hello."

"Hey, boo."

Tracey's heart skipped a beat at recognizing her man's voice. "Rafique, baby, I miss you so much. When are you coming home?"

"As soon as it cools off some. It's still too hot for me to be coming back."

As Rafique was talking, Pluck emerged from the motel room. He looked at Rafique, his face a mask of impatience. "Yo, Fique! Come on, youngin, we got to go!"

Rafique held up his index finger and continued to talk on the phone. "Look, baby, I got to go, but I'ma call you as soon as I get to where I'm going."

"No. Fuck that, Rafique. You ain't going nowhere. I ain't heard from you in three weeks and you think you just gonna talk to me for a few minutes and hang up?"

"Tracey, come on, baby, you tripping. What the fuck you think I'ma stand out here and talk to you for hours? I'ma call you later on."

Tracey became hysterical. "No, fuck that! How you just gonna be treating me like this! No, Rafique! You ain't going no fucking where!"

Rafique was just about to hang up on her when her next words stopped him cold.

"That's why I can't wait to get this baby out of me!"

Rafique was speechless. He removed the phone from his ear and stared at it as if he could see her face. Quickly, he regained his composure and put the phone back to his ear. "Tracey, you pregnant?"

Tracey responded through the sobs, "Y-y-eah."

"Look, baby, don't do nothing drastic. Wait til I come home so we can talk about this."

Tracey sniffled. "Well when you coming home? Because we need to talk about this as soon as possible."

Rafique hadn't planned on going back to Philly anytime soon. The question caught him off guard, so he said the first thing that popped into his mind: "I'll be back this weekend."

"Are you sure?"

"Yeah, I'm sure; I'll call you before I leave."

With that, they said their goodbyes and hung up. Rafique walked slowly back to his room, opened the door, and sat quietly on the bed. Pluck took one look at him and shook his head. *I can't understand this motherfucker. He talk all this shit about being on top of his game when it comes to women. But when it come to this bitch out Philly, he go stupid.* Pluck kept this thought to himself. Instead, he just asked, "What's up, youngin?"

"I just hung up the phone with Tracey. She pregnant man. I need to get back to Philly. She talking about getting an abortion. I got to talk her out of that shit. That's my child she talking about killing."

Pluck didn't respond. He just sat there thinking, *I knew that was that bitch on the phone. If he go back to Philly, he out of his motherfucking mind.* Once again, Pluck didn't express what he was thinking. He knew that Rafique had made up his mind, and once that happened, it was a done deal. Pluck knew that nothing he said would change the outcome. It would only make Rafique go into big-brother mode, and the conversation would then become condescending. So Pluck just sat there shaking his head, feeling bad for his brother.

A couple hours later they were on the road again. Rafique dropped Pluck off at his grandparent's house. As Pluck walked up the steps, Rafique called out, "Yo, Pluck!"

Pluck turned around.

"I'll be back in a little bit. I'ma go holla at my pop for a minute."

"Alright, youngin, I ain't going nowhere. I'll see you later on. Oh yeah, tell my mom I said what's up."

Rafique nodded his head, beeped his horn, and pulled off.

CHAPTER FIVE

Jamil sat in his favorite chair, which from ten years of use was molded perfectly to fit his body. At this time in his life, he was living in a small two-bedroom apartment with his wife, Lorraine, his newly born and seventh child, Ali and his stepdaughter, Lachelle. On this particular day, he was in the house alone. Lorraine and the children were at her parent's house.

With his eyes closed, his mind, body, and soul rode the waves of relaxation on the magical notes of Miles Davis as the fusion of rock-and-roll and jazz blended perfectly. The earphones blocked out all sound except that of the music as Jamil tapped his foot and nodded his head to the rich rhythms.

Miles was a bad motherfucker, he thought as the tape came to an end. Jamil got up and headed to his bookshelf. The cheap homemade bookshelf stood about six feet high and stretched a few feet from the front window to a few feet from the front door, covering one side of the wall of his front room. It was lined from top to bottom with books. On the top shelves were all of his Islamic books: Hadiths, Qurans, different Islamic philosophers,

Arabic language books, and Islamic history books. The rest of the shelves held an assortment of books about Western and African histories and civilizations. These books were his most prized possessions and the only thing he loved more than jazz.

Jamil reached up and grabbed his Quran. *I'm glad Lorraine and the kids ain't here. Now I can get some reading done.* Jamil sat back in his favorite chair and began to read. After a few minutes, though, his mind began to wander.

For the past twenty years he had been a devout Muslim. He felt like Islam was the perfect religion for black people in America. Things were a bit frustrating, though. He was the father of seven children and he had introduced them all to Islam, but none of them really accepted it. He attributed that to their youthfulness, but it still bothered him. *Shit, when I was young I wasn't like my children are. This a different time now, though. There are no Malcolm X's, no Stokely Carmichael's, no H. Rap Brown, no Panther Party. Back when I was young we had a political maturity that doesn't exist today. We were more serious. Now all they seemed to be concerned with is fucking each other, that stupid ass hippiddy hoppiddy music they be listening to, and smoking that damn cocaine.* Jamil sighed and put his book down as thoughts of his children ran through his mind. He couldn't help but to think of his middle son, Rafique. He went back to the day he had gotten a phone call and it was Rafique informing him of the trouble he was in.

"Abbee, the police are looking for me."

"For what, son?"

"They saying I killed someone."

"They what?!"

"They want me for a homicide."

"Okay son. Look, leave Philly right now. As soon as you hang up this phone, you should be on your way out here. You hear me?"

"Yeah, I hear you."

Rafique arrived in town that night. For most people in a situation like this, a parent would most likely advise their child to turn themselves in to the authorities, but not Jamil. Jamil understood what his son was up against. He understood that Rafique had put himself into the hands of a system that was fundamentally unfair, particularly for poor people and people of color. Because of the institutionalized racism that this country was plagued by, it would be virtually impossible for his son to receive fair treatment. In the eyes of the state, Rafique was guilty until proven innocent, and he just didn't have the money or the complexion that was necessary to achieve fairness. Jamil understood that justice was color-blind – in the sense that it only sees in shades of white.

Now a month later, Rafique still remained free and Jamil worried about his well-being. Jamil was very disappointed at how things had turned out for his son. Jamil knew Rafique was brilliant, but what good would that do Rafique if Rafique didn't know. Jamil shook his head as he recalled teaching Rafique how to read. He could remember when his mother finally sent Rafique to him when he was seven years old and beginning to get out of control. Jamil immediately went to work on him. By the time he went back to Philly a year later, he went from not being able to read to memorizing whole books and being able to recite them. *I guess I didn't do a good enough job with him.* Jamil was going through what most parents go through when the life of their child doesn't turn out good – they blame themselves. There was a gulf between Jamil and his son that Jamil just couldn't seem to bridge. No matter what he tried, his son just wouldn't open up to him. This was the reason Jamil blamed himself for his son's outcome in life. He was absent for most of Rafique's life. This was why his son couldn't feel comfortable around him. The only way to change this was with time, and Jamil worried that Rafique's was running out. *Damn, I need a cigarette.* Jamil searched around for his pack of Marlboro Lights. He found them in between the cushions of his couch. *Shit, I only got two left.* Jamil took out one of his last two cigarettes and lit it. *This life I've lived hasn't been a very good one. I've studied overseas for eight years, I speak Arabic and French fluently, and I still can't get a good job. My children are spread out across three states, and all of them believe I've been a father to none.*

    Jamil stubbed out his cigarette and put on his shoes. He needed some more cigarettes.

✻ ✻ ✻

Rafique turned onto the tree lined street that his father lived on. He drove carefully, not wanting to accidentally hit one of the many children that ran up and down the block. He smiled as he watched the children play, thinking about how kids could run around and not be affected by the heat.

    Rafique pulled up in front of his father's apartment building. Just as he came to a complete stop the apartment door opened up and out stepped his father. Rafique called out, "Abbee!"

    Jamil looked over, saw his son and smiled. His worries and fears somehow evaporated at seeing his son safe. Jamil was a handsome man in his mid-forties, but looked to be in his thirties. The two of them looked more like brothers than father and son.

"Yo, where you going?" Rafique asked as Jamil reached the car.

"I'm going to the store. I ran out of cigarettes."

"Get in I'll drive you."

Jamil lit up his last Marlboro Light, threw the empty pack away, and got into the car. With the air conditioner on blast, the cool confines of the air were a welcome relief from the oppressive heat as he took a drag from the cigarette.

The Brand Nubians were still playing in the car when Rafique pulled off. Jamil didn't like rap music, but he never really listened to it either. Surprisingly, he liked this particular song as he nodded his head to the beat. After about a block, Jamil turned the music down and looked at his son. "Rafique, you see those brothers on the corner?"

Rafique nodded his head, seeing a group of young men standing on the corner drinking forties.

"Well, you can leave this town and come back ten years later and those same brothers will be on that same corner doing the same thing."

"Come on, Abbee, how you know that? What, you can tell the future now?"

"I don't have to be able to read the future to be able to predict how their lives will turn out. You see, a lot of black men get to a certain age, about seventeen, and they stop growing mentally. So what you have as a result are men with the mental capacity of children. They're stuck, stagnated in their development. That's why those brothers there will always be there, stuck at seventeen, doing what seventeen-year-olds do."

Rafique was silent and listening to what his father said and at the same time thinking, *Aw here we go with this speech shit again. I knew I should've let him go to the store by his fucking self.* Rafique remained silent. He popped out his Brand Nubian tape and turned on the radio. Phyllis Hyman was on, filling the car with her heartbreaking song.

"Now that's music," Jamil said as he began to sing some of the song. He stopped and looked at his son again. "Rafique, have you been making your prayers?"

Rafique kept his eyes glued to the road. "Yeah."

Jamil knew his son was lying. "Look, son, the situation you're in, the first thing you need to do is ask Allah for his forgiveness."

Rafique didn't respond right away as an intense frustration began to mount within him. After driving along in silence for a few minutes, the frustration that had been building burst to the surface. "Abbee, I'm on the run for a murder and all you can say is pray? I need to know what to do besides turn myself in. I'm stressed out, I'm paranoid, I'm losing weight, and on top of all that my girl in Philly just told me she pregnant and talking about getting an abortion. Now I got to go back and reassure her that everything will be okay. So right now I need some practical advice to help me through this."

Jamil looked at his son and felt the frustration, the hurt, and the fear as if it were his own. "Pull over, son."

Rafique pulled over at the next light and waited for his father to speak. Jamil, knowing his son was stressed out, took that into consideration before he spoke. "Something practical, huh? Okay, don't go back to Philly. That could very well be one of the worst mistakes you can make right now. If you really think seeing this girl is gonna make a difference in what she decides to do – and make no mistake about it, this is her decision – but if you think going back to Philly will change that, think again. Why don't you just send her a train ticket so she can come to you?"

"That might be too risky. Homicide could be parked outside the house. They might follow her or something. I'd rather slip in the city and slip back out again."

"You serious ain't you? Rafique I know you're a smart man, but getting you to see it so that you can apply it is a major task. I mean, what you just said is beyond stupid. Now I let you get away with disrespecting me when I asked you about making prayer. I know you're frustrated. But I can't stand around and let you talk stupid on top of that. Come on, son, think. I'm begging you, don't go back to Philly."

Rafique, intended on doing what he wanted to do, just nodded his head and pulled off, hoping that the conversation was dead.

CHAPTER SIX

Twenty minutes after dropping his father off, Rafique was blowing the horn in front of Pluck's home. Pluck came to the door and shouted, "I'll be right out." A few minutes later, he was jogging down the steps. Pluck got into the car and shut the door. "Where we going?"

"We going back to Fort Totten," Rafique said while putting the car in drive and pulling off.

"Yo, man, is you gonna get a couple of ounces or what?"

"Naw, man, we just gonna chill." As Rafique was answering, he was pulling off North Capital Street into Fort Totten's parking lot. At the same time, White Girl Ann, who always came through to buy coke, was parking her cherry-red Benz. Rafique blew his horn, catching her attention. Ann smiled at seeing who blew the car horn at her. She waved as Rafique and Pluck got out of the car.

"What's up, Ann? Let me holla at you for a minute," Rafique said as Ann got out the car and approached them.

"Hhheeeyyy, Rafique," Ann said, still smiling.

"What's up, Ann? Listen, my brother over there is a virgin and I'm trying to get him some. What's up? I want you to take care of him."

Ann looked over at Pluck and blushed. "I'll take care of him, but this pussy ain't free."
This bitch swear she black. "What you want, man?"
"You got some coke?"
"Naw."
"Naw? Well I want fifty dollars apiece."
"Apiece? I ain't say nothing about me."
"Yeah, I know, but I been wanting to taste some of that chocolate for a while now."
"Damn, Ann, how the fuck you playing me? How you gonna charge me for something you want?"
"Alright, boo, calm down. You can't hate a bitch for trying," Ann said, rolling her green eyes and shifting her weight from one wide hip to the other.
"You better stop playing all the time."
"Yeah, whatever. Is y'all ready or what?"
"Yeah we ready. Yo, Pluck! Come on man!"
Pluck jogged to catch up to Rafique and Ann. Rafique turned to him. "Yo, you got any rubbers?" Pluck looked at Ann with a hunger in his eyes that made Ann a little nervous. Pluck pulled out a pack of rubbers. "Yeah, I got some."
Ann looked at Pluck, her anxiety level increasing. "Rafique, what's up with your brother? Why he looking all crazy?" Ann whispered into Rafique's ear.
Rafique laughed out loud. "Yo, man, the motherfucker horny, that's all. He cool, relax. Ay, Pluck! Yo, you scaring her bro, stop looking all crazy."
Pluck snapped out of it. "Huh?"
"Yo, come on, man." Rafique led the way to the first building of the complex, which was abandoned.
Inside the building, they took the stairs one flight down to the laundry room in the basement. The darkened

basement had a mildew smell from the damp, bacteria-infected floors and walls. Trash was thrown everywhere from people using the abandoned building for a dump. Empty cocaine bags, burnt-out matches, hypodermic needles, and condoms littered the ground from the crackheads, dope fiends, and prostitutes coming inside to get away from prying eyes and bad weather.

Ann walked up to Rafique and grabbed him in the crotch. "Yo, Ann, I'm cool. This thing is for my brother."

"You sure? Cause I got enough for both of y'all."

"Yeah, Ann, I'm cool. I got you though. Make sure you take care of him."

Ann nodded her head and looked over to Pluck. She beckoned him to come to her with her index finger. Pluck eagerly approached Ann with a condom in his hand. Ann dropped to her knees and held her hand out. Pluck gave Ann the rubber and stared at her. Ann took control. She took the rubber out of its package and placed it in her mouth. Pluck starred in amazement as Ann blew air in the rubber and then pushed her tongue in it. Ann wasted no time as she grabbed Pluck and put the rubber on with her mouth. Pluck closed his eyes, tilted his head back, and let out a low moan. Rafique stood off to the side laughing; he was imagining what Pluck was going through at that moment.

After about five minutes, Pluck suddenly told Ann to stop. He pulled back and took off the rubber and his shirt. Pluck tossed the rubber to the floor and laid his shirt on the floor, too. Rafique stood by, puzzled. *What the fuck is Pluck doing?* To his surprise, Pluck asked Ann to take her clothes off. He grabbed her hand and guided her to the shirt. Ann taking his lead, laid her back onto his shirt that was on the floor. *What the fuck is this crazy motherfucker doing?* Rafique couldn't believe his eyes as Pluck began to get undressed. *Oh shit! This nigga getting buck ass naked.* Rafique stood in utter shock as Pluck took off every stitch of clothing he had on. The mystery was over as Rafique watched his brother lie on top of Ann to make passionate love to her.

"Who pussy is this?" Pluck gasped out.

"It's yours, baby," Ann whispered back.

"Who fucks the best, me or my brother?"

"You do, baby. Oooohhhh, you do."

Rafique couldn't believe what he was seeing. *Pluck is fucking crazy.* This was Rafique's thought right before he burst into a fit of laughter. Oblivious to Rafique and how amused he was, Pluck and Ann kept right at it.

Rafique was laughing so hard that his stomach began to ache. He had to get out of there, so he left.

After about twenty minutes Pluck came out of the laundry room, face covered in sweat with nothing on but his boxers. Rafique took one look at him and the laughter came bursting out again. Pluck was puzzled, "Yo, man, what the fuck you laughing at?"

In between laughs, Rafique responded, "Nigga, you crazy."

Pluck put his pants on, still looking puzzled. He shook his head and headed up the stairs. Rafique waited for Ann, paid her when she came out the room, and they both left the building. All three were headed to the middle building: Ann to buy some cocaine, Pluck to hang out, and Rafique to see his girl.

The young hustlers were out in full force and the human traffic was thick as crackheads hustled up and down the walkway buying coke.

One of the residents of the middle building had placed a speaker in the window and turned the volume up, blasting the music of the go-go band, Rare Essence. Their front man, Stinky Dink, rapped effortlessly over the pounding African congos.

STINKY DINK, GET RICKETY RAW,
STINKY DINK, GET RICKETY RAW…..

Aisha was sitting in her favorite beach chair and nodding her head in time with the beat. She smiled at seeing Rafique and Pluck approach. She stood up, locked her knees back, and welcomed her man with open arms and a passionate kiss. After the kiss, Rafique leaned to the side and whispered into her ear, "Listen, baby, I'm going to Philly this weekend."

Aisha backed away and frowned. "Are you taking me with you? I want to meet your family, especially your daughter."

"Naw, Eesh, I can't take you with me now. It's kind of fucked up back there right now. I'm going through some serious shit with some niggas, and shit could get out of control. If something were to happen to you, I'd be fucked up. I'll only be gone for a couple days. Plus I'ma stay with you til I leave."

"Baby, why don't you just stay with me? I don't know why you be wanting to stay in that fucked up motel anyway."

"Eesh, I would love to stay with you, but right now I just need to be by myself. It ain't got nothing to do with you, so don't think that. It's just that I need to get some things right with me and I can't do that here."

Rafique stared deep into her eyes to cement the lie he was telling. He couldn't take her back to Philly – Tracey definitely wasn't going for that – and he still hadn't told her he was a fugitive and that was the reason he chose to stay at the motel. Rafique grabbed her hand. "Let's go inside, I feel like sweating."

Aisha liked what she had just heard. She blushed, turned around, and walked seductively to her apartment with Rafique right on her heels.

CHAPTER SEVEN

A few days later, Rafique was on 95 North taking the two-hour trip back to Philadelphia, the City Of Brotherly Love. Arriving in town, he headed straight for South Philly where his best friend Shawn lived. Shawn stayed on Delhi Street, right off 11th and Fitzwater.

Rafique pulled up to his friend's home. He noticed that the lights were on. *Good, someone's home.* Rafique parked, got out, grabbed his Nike duffle bag of clothes and cosmetics, shut the car door, and walked down the small treeless street to Shawn's front door.

Rafique rang the doorbell and waited for a couple of minutes before a woman's voice answered, "Who is it?" It was Ari, Shawn's baby's mother.

"It's Rafique."

The lock to the door clicked and the door opened. Ari stood in the doorway looking fine as ever. She had light skin and her jet black hair was pulled back in a long ponytail. Her almond-shaped eyes sparkled with joy at seeing Rafique. "Hhheeyyy Rafique," she said, giving him a warm embrace.

"What's up, girl. Damn, look at you looking all good. Step back and let me get a good look at your fine ass."

"Boy, stop playing and come on in," Ari responded laughing lightly.

"Where Shawn at?"

"He upstairs putting Diva to sleep."

"Could you let him know I'm down here?"

Ari turned around and headed up the steps. Rafique made himself at home. He turned on the television and took a seat on the couch. Shawn came walking down the steps a few minutes later. "Damn nigga, what's up Fique?"

"What's up Shawn?"

The two friends, happy to see one another, shook hands and embraced. They had been friends since the sixth grade. Including Rafique and Shawn, there were ten of them in their little squad: Tashi, Rick, Dave, Snag, Cook, Speed, Dry, and Manchild. Coming up, they did everything together, forging a bond that over the years stretched but remained intact. As they became older they slowly began to go their separate ways. With children of their own, girlfriends, and jobs that took up most their time, they couldn't hang out like they used to when they were younger. Most of Rafique's friends had slowed down, conforming to their responsibilities, but not Rafique. He continued to play the game, which was the reason he was now sneaking back into town.

"What the fuck you doing back in town? You know motherfuckers is saying that nigga Fuzz gave you up?"

"Yeah, I heard. But, Shawn, man you know me. You know I wouldn't do nothing with nobody I ain't really fuck with."

"Yeah. But when you high Rafique, the same rules don't apply. You know that."

"Yeah, man, and that's what's fucked up about this whole situation. Man, I can't remember nothing about that night."

The two friends were silent for a moment, deep in their thought. Rafique was attempting to recall the memory that still eluded him and Shawn was trying to figure out why Rafique was back in town, knowing the police were after him. Shawn broke the silence by voicing these thoughts: "Fique, what the fuck you doing back?"

Rafique couldn't look Shawn in the eye. He found a spot on the floor and focused on it. Rafique knew he was doing something stupid and he was ashamed. He also knew that Shawn was going to check him for it. "Tracey told me she pregnant."

"Rafique, I asked you why you was back in town? What do Tracey being pregnant have to do wi...hold the fuck up, I know you ain't come back because of that. Nigga, is you crazy? I know you ain't come back about no bitch."

"Naw, man, it ain't just about her. She carrying my child and talking about destroying it. I can't let that happen."

"Yo, man, what the fuck is wrong with you? You can't see through that shit? That bitch got you open like that? Man, she just trying to get you back so she can see you, selfish bitch. She probably ain't even pregnant."

Rafique was silent as Shawn continued to talk.

"But you know what? If she is, if she ain't, it don't even matter. Nigga, your life is on the line. If you in jail, then what? What good can you be to a baby in jail? If she get an abortion, then it really don't matter."

Rafique stood silently, still focused on that spot on the floor. He knew that Shawn was right. His father had been telling him the same thing. But right now he wasn't ready to admit it. He became defensive. Rafique looked him dead in the eye. His voice shook, betraying the anger he tried to conceal. "Nigga, I do what the fuck I want to do.

If I go to jail, ain't nobody gonna do the time but me. So leave me the fuck alone about the decisions I make and stop calling my girl a bitch!"

Shawn chose his next words carefully. He shook his head and held Rafique's gaze. "Fique, you my man and you right, ain't nobody going to do that time but you. I got love for you though, and I don't want to see you do time at all. So when I see you making questionable moves, I'ma say something. I don't give a fuck if you get mad. Nigga, I'm obligated to say something and I would expect the same thing from you if I was in your position."

"Is you finished nigga? Where the phone at?"

"You know where the fucking phone at. I'm going back upstairs."

Shawn turned and left Rafique standing where he was. Rafique stood there a moment watching Shawn before he walked off to the kitchen to use the phone. He picked it up and dialed his apartment. Tracey picked up after a few rings. "Hello."

"Hey baby, how's my girl?"

"Rafique! Please tell me you're back."

"Yeah, baby, I'm back."

"So when can I see you?"

"Right now if you want."

"You know I do. Are you coming home?"

"Come on now, don't be stupid. Didn't you tell me the police be parked outside the house?"

"Yeah, but they ain't been out here in while."

"Alright, look, this what I need you to do. Get you a cab to 11th and Fitzwater. I'ma meet you there. Pack you up some clothes for the weekend. You dressed?"

"Yeah."

"Hold on."

Rafique used the three-way to call the cab company. When he clicked back to Tracey, the phone was ringing.

"Baby, who you calling?"

"I'm calling a cab."

When the cab dispatch answered after a few rings, Tracey gave him her address and destination and thanked him. Rafique clicked him off the line. They continued to talk as Tracey packed. Fifteen minutes later there was a car honking outside the apartment.

"Rafique, the cab is out front blowing the horn."

"Alright, go ahead, I'll be waiting on you when you get here."

Rafique hung up the phone. He waited for ten minutes before heading for the door. "Yo, Shawn, I'm out. I'm going to the North American. I'll see you in a couple days."

Shawn heard Rafique and came halfway down the steps. "Alright, homes. Yo, be careful out there man."

"Alright, I'ma call you later on."

As Rafique headed out the door, he thought about what Shawn said about coming back to Philly but quickly disregarded it. He got into the car and drove one block to 11th and Fitzwater, parked, and waited for the cab to show up. Ten minutes later, the cab pulled up on the opposite corner. After paying the cabbie, Tracey got out and looked around for her man. Rafique waited and watched for ten minutes before blowing the horn and hitting his high beams. Tracey heard the horn and saw the lights. She quickly walked over to the car. "Rafique, you was here all that time?" she asked while getting into the car.

"Yeah, I was here. I was just making sure you wasn't followed."

After sliding over and kissing her man passionately, Tracey stared at Rafique before asking, "Baby, where you taking me?'

"Just sit back and relax. We'll be there in minute."

Rafique pulled off and drove at the speed limit. He couldn't afford to get pulled over after all this time on the run. It would be a crime to go to jail for speeding. Rafique kept his eyes on the road. "Tracey, turn on W.D.A.S. The Quiet Storm is on."

Tracey did as she was asked, filling the car with the perfect harmonies of Force MD's.

AS THE SUN SETS,
AND THE NIGHT COMES ARRROOUUNNDDD,
I CAN FEEL MY EMOTION COME DOOOWWNNN....

Their 1980's hit "Tears" played as the theme of the Quiet Storm, thunder and rain mingled faintly in the background. Tracey snuggled close and chuckled lightly as Rafique tried to match the lead singer's tenor rifts.

Twenty minutes later they were pulling up into North American's parking lot. Rafique grabbed the bags as Tracey got the room. Once in the room, Tracey rushed into Rafique's arms. She whispered into his ear, "Damn, baby, I missed you so much."

Tracey placed a wet kiss on his mouth and squeezed him tight. She paused. "Baby, I was sick not having you around."

"I know, Tray. But you know it's dangerous for me to be back here. I'm taking a hell of a risk."

"I know, baby. Please forgive me for being so selfish, but like I said, I need you."

"It's okay, I'm here now."

They renewed their kissing with a bit more desire. At the same time, Tracey reached down and began massaging Rafique.

"Slow down baby, I need to take a shower. Plus, you know, the weekend ain't gonna end in the next couple minutes."

Tracey reluctantly stopped, and Rafique walked to the bathroom.

The steaming, hot water felt refreshing as all the pent-up tensions from the past few months seemed to magically dissipate from his body. With his eyes closed and head under the shower nozzle, he was in a state of total relaxation. At that moment, the shower curtain opened. Tracey stood still with nothing on but a towel wrapped around her and a seductive look in her eyes.

"You was taking so long I had to see what was keeping you." Tracey let the towel drop and slowly did a pirouette so that his eyes could drink in all the nuances and the beauty of her body.

"Damn, I see that ass got a little fatter. What you been climbing one of them stairmasters since I've been gone?"

"Stairmaster? That shit for them white girls. This here all me." Tracey slowly spent, giving Rafiqe another look before she stepped into the shower. "Mommy needs to be taken care of now." She closed the shower curtain behind her and began kissing him on the chest. Her tongue and lips did an exotic dance down his body, raising the temperature in the shower to an unbearable degree.

After serious lovemaking, the two of them wrapped up in each other's arms and talked. "Tracey, what's up with the baby?"

"Rafique, there's nothing in this world that I would want more than to have your baby."

"So what was all that shit you was talking on the phone?"

"Baby, you know I wouldn't do no shit like that. I could never kill our child. It's just that I was sick not having you here with me, and I figured if I said I was getting an abortion you would come home."

"Hold up, you mean to tell me you took advantage of how I feel about abortions, knowing I might risk coming back here to stop you. Man, you allowed me to put my freedom on the line about some dick! What the fuck is wrong with you? What if I got locked up, then what? Did you think about that?"

Tears flowed freely down her face as she choked back the sobs. "Baby, I'm sorry. Please forgive me. I know I was wrong and I was being selfish. I never even thought about you going to jail. All I could think about was having you here with me."

Rafique knew all along that she just wanted to see him and although hearing it upset him, he didn't stay angry long. He couldn't heap all the blame on her. He wanted to come back just as bad as she wanted him to. He missed Philly, but most of all, he missed her. So, against his better judgment and the advice of his father and Shawn, he used the excuse of an abortion to come back.

The two lovers spent the next day and a half holed up in their room, only leaving out to eat. Finally, Sunday night had arrived and it was time for him to go back. With Tracey asleep in his arms, he gently shook her awake. "Baby, the honeymoon is over; it's time for me to go."

Tracey yawned and laid her head on his chest. As the tears welled up in her eyes, she whispered softly in his ear, "Baby, these last couple days have been so good for me. They just went by so fast. I wish we could stay like this forever. When will I see you again?" Tracey couldn't hold back the tears any longer. They fell uncontrollably down her face.

"When I get to where I'm going. I'll call you and let you know."

"Rafique, why can't you let me know where you're staying?"

"Because you can't tell what you don't know."

Rafique's answer cut Tracey deep. But in a way she understood. It was the paranoia, but that didn't stop the sobs as she buried her face in his chest and the tears continued to flow.

After waiting for a cab to pick Tracey up, Rafique hit the road, heading back to DC. Before he got to the highway, Rafique cruised slowly through the Philadelphia streets. As the scenery flashed by in his peripheral, he noticed a man and a boy playing catch while a woman stood by and watched. That scene made Rafique think of Tracey and his unborn child and what, if any, kind of life he could provide for them being a fugitive.

CHAPTER EIGHT

Back at the motel room, Rafique lay on his back while contemplating his next move. He was running short on money again. After thinking for a few minutes, he stepped outside to the pay phone – he needed to call Andre.

Andre was Rafique's friend who lived down the street from his father's house. Andre was a six-foot-one, two hundred-pound seventeen-year-old who didn't have the sense he was born with. Within the past year, Andre had gotten his hands on a rusty 9mm handgun. To this day, Rafique didn't know where he got it from – Dre refused to tell him – but ever since that day, Andre had become a different person.

Like most inner-city children, Andre's world was ruled by material possessions. A vacuum created by powerlessness was filled with the trappings of symbols of success. The cars, the jewelry, the clothes, the women, these symbols represented identity. To have none of these things destroyed confidence. Andre was one those people who lacked confidence. To his peers, Andre was just big, goofy, and dirty. All that changed, though, when Andre got that gun.

From the first time Andre saw the look of fear that a gun in someone's face could provoke, he was a different man. The first time he got a taste of the power that his gun gave him, he became intoxicated by it. Prior to having a gun he was a boy with no confidence; now he felt like Superman, who had the power of life and death in his hands. Andre became dangerous and unpredictable, and Rafique took a chance that something could go terribly wrong every time he called him to get some money. At this time in his life, though, Rafique didn't care. Whatever he had to do to keep his head above water, he would do. And if that included the potential of Andre doing something crazy, so be it.

"Hello." Andre picked up after one ring.

"Hello, can I speak to Andre?"

"This Dre. Who this, Rafique?"

"Yeah. What's up, Dre?"

"What's up, Joe."

"I'm just trying to figure out how I'ma get me some ones. I'ma little fucked up right now."

"You know what, youngin, I know these bamas from New York. They just opened up shop on Galatin Street."

Without asking, Rafique immediately knew why Dre mentioned the New Yorkers. "Oh yeah? Is they strapped?"

"Yeah, but you can easily get the drop on 'em. These stupid-ass bamas be leaving they guns in the bedroom."

"Man, how you know all this?"

"Well, you know me, I started buying a little coke off 'em just to see what kind of numbers they was doing. I got cool with 'em, and them stupid-ass bamas let me see everything I needed to see."

"So what's a good time to holla at these motherfuckers?"

"Probably like late Saturday night."

Rafique was with it. Anything to put some money in his pockets was a go. This was why he called Andre. Rafique knew that Andre was going to have a way to get some money in his pockets.

Rafique and Andre schemed for more than an hour on how to pull the robbery off before they hung up. Rafique stretched, he was bored. With nothing planned for the rest of the day, he laid down on his bed and stared at the ceiling. His mind was blank for a moment before he started thinking about his little brother and sisters. *I know what I'ma do. I'ma go see my little brother and sisters.* Rafique had two little sisters and a brother who stayed with their mother in the Southeast section of DC. His father had been separated from their mother for the past five years, so Rafique didn't see his siblings as much as he used to. With something to do now, he got up, got dressed, and was out the door on his way to Southeast. It took him twenty minutes to arrive at their home. It was the middle of the afternoon and the sun was at its apex. It was blazing hot outside, the neighborhood was quiet, and the streets were empty. Rafique got out of the car and was immediately engulfed by the heat. *It's hot as a motherfucker out here.* The heat seemed to seep through his pores and rob him of his strength. It was a labor just walking half a block to their front door. He knocked hard and waited patiently for someone to answer. A few seconds went by before the muffled voice of a young girl could be heard through the door. "Who is it?"

"It's me your big brother."

The lock to the door clicked, the door swung open and a beautiful little girl leapt into his arms. "Rafique!"

"Hey, Jibah. How's my favorite little sister?"

"I'm fine."

"Where Muhammed and Nafisah at?"

"In the house."

Najibah was the youngest of three of his father's children by his former wife Nailah. Muhammed was twelve, and Nafisah was seventeen. It was still early in the day as he sat around and played with his siblings. "Ay, y'all, y'all want to go to the movies?"

"Yeah," they all replied in unison.

"Alright, go get dressed."

While they were busy getting dressed Rafique picked up the phone and called his father to ask him if he wanted to go. Jamil agreed and Rafique hung up. Not too long after that, the children were ready.

On the ride to pick up his father, Rafique started thinking about family and how important it was to him. He had brothers and sisters spread out over three states. One of his goals in life was to try to get them all together and really strengthen the bonds that time and space had strained.

They arrived at their father's house just as the sun was beginning to set. Rafique blew the horn and waited. Jamil came right out and jogged to the car.

"Get in the back Nafisah," Jamil said, opening the car door.

Nafisah got out the car and got into the back seat. Once in the car, Jamil turned to Rafique and said, "Put on some of that rap music y'all be listening to." Although Jamil didn't like rap music, in an attempt to relate to his son, he asked to hear it.

Rafique reached over in the glove compartment and pulled out KRS One's "You Must Learn." He popped it into the tape deck, turned the volume up, and pulled off. With KRS pumping from the sound system, Rafique glanced at his father and smiled. Jamil was nodding his head to the beat.

After the song went off, Jamil chuckled. "Now put on some of that real rap y'all be listening to."

"What you mean real rap? That was real rap. KRS is one of my favorite rappers."

"You know what I mean."

Rafique waited until he came to a red light. He looked into the glove compartment and pulled out NWA's "Straight Outta Compton." He replaced KRS One in the tape deck.

FUCK THE POLICE COMING STRAIGHT FROM THE UNDERGROUND, A YOUNG NIGGA GOT IT BAD CAUSE I'M BROWN….

Jamil clearly enjoyed what he was hearing. He had a huge smile on his face as he listened to the hip hop group out of Los Angeles that was expressing the rage of millions of black youth who constantly felt the oppressive heel of the Gestapo-like police force in inner cities across America.

"Shit, I like that. You know we had some boys back in the day used to rap like that called the Last Poets."

Rafique's response was a simple nod of his head. At this point in their relationship, father and son didn't relate well with one another. You see, Rafique was basically raised by his mother, only spending time with his father when he was too much for his mother to handle. As a result of this dynamic, Rafique equated his father with bad behavior and punishment. Because of this, Rafique up to this point, just couldn't seem to get at a comfort level with his father. The only time they even had conversations that consisted of more than a couple words were when Rafique was upset or intoxicated.

By the time they reached Georgetown where the movie was located, the sun had retreated behind the horizon, chased by the blackness of night. The movie they went to see, John Singleton's *Boyz In The Hood,* was starting in five minutes. The family got out the car and hurriedly walked to the movie theatre.

Two hours later the movie was over and they were on the way home. Jamil was feeling good because *Boyz In The Hood* had that affect on him, and he wanted to discuss what they had just seen. "What y'all think about the movie?"

"It was corny," Muhammed said.

"I liked it," Nafisah joined in.

"So did I," Najibah also said.

Rafique wanted to get on his father's nerves so he took his time before saying, "You know what? That movie let me know what I been missing in my life."

"And what might that be?" Jamil asked.

"A relationship with my father," Rafique answered, eyes glued to the road.

Jamil didn't want to have that kind of conversation in front of the children so he didn't respond, and the car remained in silence the rest of the way home.

CHAPTER NINE

The following day on his way back to his motel room, Rafique began to think of his daughter. He hadn't spoken to or seen her since he left town. He missed his little girl and he wondered how she was doing. Tired of wondering, he pulled over at the next phone booth and dialed her number. The phone rang twice before her mother, Veronica, answered. "Hello."

"Hello, Ronnie, is my daughter home?"

"Yeah, hold on a minute."

Veronica was Rafique's childhood sweetheart. He met her on his sixteenth birthday through his friend Dave. At the time, Dave was seeing her sister. On this night, Dave and Cooke, another one of Rafique's friends, were hanging out over at Rafique's house, celebrating his birthday.

"Ay, Fique, I got this girl for you. I fuck with her sister. I can call 'em up right now and they'll come over. What's up?"

"I'm cool, Dave. You know I don't fuck around with no blind dates. Call 'em up though, Cook might want her."

Dave picked up the phone and called his girl. After talking for a few minutes, Rafique overheard Dave give his girl his address. So, actually the day he met Veronica, she was a blind date for his friend Cook.

Rafique was attracted to Ronnie at first sight. She was beautiful: smooth honey-brown complexion, almond-shaped eyes, and long brown hair. Rafique could still picture her as she walked through his mother's front door. It was February and bitterly cold outside, but she was dressed for it. Her red Gerry ski jacket was zipped up to her chin. She had on some black Calvin Klein jeans that clung to her body like a second skin, with size Six, cream colored Timberland boots. Ronnie looked Rafique dead in the eyes and smiled. Rafique smiled back and made up his mind right then and there that she would be his. He leaned over to Cook. "Yo, man, sis keep gritting on me. I think she on me. Let me go at her."

Cook shrugged his shoulders, giving Rafique the green light. Rafique didn't hesitate. Playing host, he spoke, "Damn, Dave, is you gonna introduce your friends or what?"

"Oh, yeah. Derrell, Ronnie, this my man Rafique. This his house, and that's my other homie, Cook."

Both girls spoke. Ronnie never took her eyes off Rafique.

"You like what you see?" Rafique asked.

Ronnie blushed.

"Come sit right here," Rafique said indicating a spot next to him on the couch.

Ronnie approached.

"Damn, my fault, let me get your coat," Rafique said, as he stood up.

Ronnie took her coat off and handed it to Rafique and sat down.

Rafique took her coat. "Derrell, right? Let me get your coat, too," Rafique said to Ronnie's sister. Derrell took her coat off and handed it to Rafique as he walked pass her to the closet. He hung up the coats returned back to the sofa and reclaimed his seat next to Ronnie. "Like I said, do you like what you see?"

Ronnie nodded her head. "What's your name again?

"Rafique."

"What, you a mooslim or something?"

"Naw, my father is. He gave me that name. It means friend in Arabic. Something I would very much like to be to you."

"I ain't got no problem with that." Ronnie smiled again and from that point on, she had him.

With the ice broken, they began to talk, getting to know one another. He learned that she was fourteen and she didn't have a boyfriend. On that night, the first tenuous bonds were formed that Rafique believed would only get stronger and last forever.

Everyday for a month they were inseparable. With their hormones raging out of control, they were playing a grown-up game of house, too young to understand that there were consequences for every action, the kind of consequences that would last a lifetime.

Rafique was playing the role of a grown man with all the answers. He would soon find out, though, that he really understood nothing and that life didn't always go as he believed it would. Although he thought that he and Ronnie were good, life would throw him a curveball that he would miss badly.

It happened at the height of his romantic bliss. He had been sitting over at Ronnie's house as he always did at the same time. They were hugged up, listening to the radio. The doorbell rang. Ronnie got up to answer the door. She came back seconds later.

"Who was that at the door?"

"Nobody. It was for my uncle."

No soon as those words left her mouth, the bell was ringing again. Ronnie got up to answer the door once more.

This time when she came back, she wasn't alone. A guy Rafique had never seen before trailed her.

"I told you my uncle wasn't here," Ronnie said to the strange guy.

The guy just looked at Ronnie. "Yeah, alright." The guy turned to leave, but paused first. He and Ronnie exchanged looks and smiled at one another.

Rafique saw the exchanged looks and was crushed. He had no proof, so it could've been what it appeared to be – just a look. But what he saw in Ronnie's eyes and what her smile represented was betrayal. The look lasted for a brief moment in time, but the repercussions would last a lifetime. The guy turned and left and Rafique wasted no time. As soon as the door shut, he got up and prepared to leave as well.

"Rafique, where you going?"

"I'm out, man. I saw how you looked at that dude. You fucking with him, Ronnie?"

"Rafique, that's my uncle's friend. You tripping. I don't mess with that boy."

"Yeah, whatever."

Rafique grabbed his jacket and turned to leave. Ronnie tried to prevent him from going, but no matter what she said or did, she couldn't stop him.

After that night, he was never the same when it came to women. Ronnie hurt him that night, and for days afterward he suffered from the disease of a broken heart. He couldn't eat, he couldn't sleep, and for a while all he could think about was her. It took him some time to get over her, but once he did, he wasn't the same. His trust in women had been destroyed and it wouldn't heal for a long time after that.

It wasn't too long after that night that he found out Ronnie was pregnant. She called him one day with the news. "Rafique, I'm pregnant."

There was a pause.

"Rafique!"

"What?"

"I'm like two months pregnant."

"And you telling me because…"

"I'm telling you because you the father."

"No, I think you need to tell your fucking boyfriend."

After the break-up, Ronnie had hooked up with the same guy she claimed had been her uncle's friend.

"Rafique, you know this your baby. You told me I was pregnant."

"Come on, man, how the fuck would I know you was pregnant? I was just saying that cause it was feeling good. Look man, I'ma about to leave out, so stop calling me with this shit!" Rafique hung the phone up.

Afterward, he did the math and realized that he could be the father. Rafique let a couple days pass before he called her back. He admitted to her that he could very well be the father. Throughout her pregnancy he tried to reconcile their fractured relationship, but it was to no avail. Rafique's attitude towards women had disintegrated into one of "fuck bitches." He had lost all respect and trust. Even after his little girl was born with his face and he held that beautiful, new precious life in his arms, that attitude and his immaturity strained his relationship with Ronnie so much so that they barely spoke to one another.

Now six years later as he waited for his little girl to get on the phone, they still barely spoke.

"Shante, your dad is on the phone," Ronnie said without another word to Rafique.

"Hello? Hi, Dad."

"Hhheeyyy, how's my little princess?"

"Fine."

"You miss me?'

"Yeah."

As Rafique talked to his daughter, Rafique could feel the distance between them as if it were a physical barrier. He realized at that moment that he was repeating the same mistakes his father had made with him. He made a promise to himself that day on the phone: whenever this situation – with him being a fugitive – died down, he would do everything in his power to prevent the relationship with his daughter to end up like the one he had with his father.

Rafique talked to his daughter for a few more minutes and then hung up. He jumped back into his car, but instead of going back to his motel room, he changed direction and headed to Aisha's.

CHAPTER TEN

Rafique stepped out of Aisha's apartment into the beaming rays of sunlight. He shielded his eyes and took a look around. Besides a few young men sitting on the steps smoking a joint, it was one of those rare occasions when traffic at Fort Totten was light.

"Yo, Fique," one of the young men sitting on the steps said. He coughed as the marijuana smoke irritated his lungs.

"This youngin was up here looking for you."

"Who was it?" Rafique asked.

"I don't know. Some big bama-ass nigga. I ain't ask his name."

That probably was Dre. "Alright, good looking out." Rafique started down the steps. "How long ago was that?"

"Bout ten, fifteen minutes."

"Alright, Jon-Jon. Good looking out."

Rafique quickly walked to his car and took the five minute drive to Andre's house.

Andre hated the young men from Fort Totten. Most of his negative feelings came from jealousy and the fact that they use to treat Andre with a bit of contempt. You see,

Fort Totten was a spot that generated money, and most of the young men who lived in those projects hustled. This provided them with materials that gave them a feeling of superiority over those who could not afford those materials. Andre was one of those guys. But since Andre got that gun, his attitude was one of: the Fort Totten young men were cowards and they didn't deserve anything that they hustled for. Especially, if they couldn't stop Andre from taking it from them. The only reason why Andre didn't move on his feelings was because of Rafique. If not for Rafique, he would've been moved out and caused all types of havoc in Fort Totten.

Rafique spotted Andre as soon as he turned the corner onto his block. Rafique pulled up and double-parked in front of Andre's door. He rolled his window down. "What's up, Dre?" He could tell by the facial expression that Dre was upset.

"Fuck them bamas, Joe!" Dre said, brandishing his rusty 9mm.

"Hoooo, Dre, what the fuck is up? Put that away and get in the car."

Dre put the gun up and got in the car. "Youngin, I went up there looking for you. And them bamas act like they ain't know who you was."

"Come on, man, is you serious? Look, them dudes don't know you like that. You could be coming up there to kill me or something. They only did what they was supposed to do."

"Them bamas jive, like, disrespected me, Joe. I just want to smoke one of them motherfuckers."

"Yo, man, is you listening? I just told you they was looking out for me. That's why I'm here now. They told me you was up there. Look in the glove compartment and pull out that weed. Light it up and calm the fuck down."

Andre mumbled incoherently to himself, got the weed, then rolled and lit it up. After a few drags, his mood and the color of his eyes changed dramatically. His eyes were blood-shot red and opened only to slits. As the weed continued to take hold, he began to act real silly. He had a big grin on his face as he turned the volume to the car stereo up. His head began to nod to the NWA pumping from the speakers. Rafique turned the radio back down. "Yo, you ready for tomorrow?"

"I been ready, Joe."

"You got some money?"

"Naw, I'm fucked up."

"Well, here you go." Rafique pulled out some money. "I got a couple dollars for you." Rafique counted out three twenties. "I'm a little fucked up, too. This all I can stand right now." Rafique handed Dre the money.

Dre took the money. "This cool, good looking out." Dre got out the car. "Alright, Joe, I'ma see you tomorrow." Andre closed the car door and walked up the steps to his home.

Rafique put the car in drive and pulled off heading back to Aisha's house.

The next night, sitting in the basement of Andre's house, Rafique, Dre, and Dre's friend Qua went over the plan once more.

"So, Dre, remember you go to the house with some weed. Smoke some with 'em, but don't inhale that shit. We don't need you all high. Remember, man, have all them niggas in the front room with you. Me and Qua gonna be there about a half hour after that. Once I knock on the door and they open it, we coming in guns drawn, laying everybody down. Qua, you duct tape everybody. Yeah, you getting duct taped too, Dre. Once that's done, we gonna get them niggas to show us where the money at." As Rafique spoke, the adrenaline began coursing through his veins, preparing his body for the upcoming robbery.

The plan went just as expected. Rafique had to hit one of the dudes in the head with his gun a couple times, drawing blood, before the guy told them where the money was. After making sure everyone was secure in the front room, they went to the bedroom to get the money. Rafique and Qua entered the bedroom and the first thing that they saw was a beautiful young women lying on the bed with the covers pulled up to her chin. It was obvious the girl was scared as her eyes darted back and forth between Rafique and Qua. Qua walked over to the bed and snatched the covers off her. The girl was naked. Qua stared at the girl hungrily and blew out a low whistle. "Goddamn girl, you fine!"

Rafique shook his head and instructed the girl, "Get up and walk over to the dresser." Rafique kept his eyes on the girl. "Yo, go check under the bed," he then said to Qua.

Qua reluctantly peeled his eyes off the girl and headed to the bed. He got on his hands and knees and peered underneath. Seconds later, he reached under the bed and pulled out two sneaker boxes. He opened them up, revealing the contents. One was full of cocaine, the other money. Qua emptied the boxed into a bag and got up off his knees.

Rafique nodded towards the girl. "Yo, keep an eye on her while I look around." Rafique walked straight over to the bed and flipped the mattress. Two guns, perfect.

One .380 and one 50 caliber Desert Eagle. Rafique tucked the 50 and tossed the .380 and his 9mm to Qua. He then began checking the dresser drawers, finding some more cash and some jewelry.

"Ay Joe, that bitch is bad ain't she?" Qua asked, looking at the girl as if she was a piece of meat and he was dying of hunger.

Rafique looked at Qua. *This nigga tripping.* Qua didn't notice how Rafique was looking at him; he was busy roughly feeling her up. The young woman was scared. You could see her body visibly shaking. The young woman looked at Rafique, her eyes pleading for help. Rafique had seen enough as he walked quickly towards Qua. "Yo man, what the fuck is you doing?"

"I'm ready to fuck this bitch, youngin," Qua responded as he resumed violating the frightened young woman.

Rafique was in arm's range as he raised his hand and tapped Qua in the head with his gun. "Look, you nut-ass nigga, we came here to get this money, not rape no motherfucking body."

Qua rubbed his head. A look of stupidity was plastered across his face. "My fault, Joe."

Rafique snatched the phone cord out the wall and then followed Qua out of the bedroom. On the way out the apartment, Qua kicked Dre in the ribs for added effect. The plan after that was to meet back at Dre's house. Dre arrived two hours later angry at Qua. "What the fuck you kick me for Joe?"

"Aw, youngin, I was just trying to make that shit look good. Plus, I ain't even hit you hard."

"Dre, how the fuck was the bitch in the bedroom? I told you to make sure everybody was in the front room."

"Fique, man, I ain't know she was there. I couldn't search the crib. How the fuck was I supposed to know she was back there?"

"Shit, we lucky the bitch was too scared to think. Yo, your man Qua over there, that nigga a nut. You know this silly motherfucker was getting ready to get a rape?"

"Damn Qua, what the fuck is up with you?" Dre asked. He stared at Qua as if he was really seeing him for the first time.

"Aw, youngin, you would've probably tried to fuck that bad motherfucker, too."

Rafique shook his head. *That sick motherfucker ain't got to worry about getting no money with me no more.*

After splitting the money, drugs, and jewelry up, Rafique tossed Dre his 9mm. He kept the 50 caliber for himself. He then got on the phone and called Pluck. "Yo, Pluck," Rafique said when Pluck got on the phone, "meet me at Eesh's in like fifteen minutes. I got something for you."

"Alright, youngin."

Rafique hung up the phone. With a pocket full of money, a couple ounces of cocaine, a new gun, and a couple pieces of jewelry, Rafique felt a lot better than he did at the beginning of the day. He shook Dre's and Qua's hand and left. Ten minutes later he was walking up the steps to Aisha's apartment building.

Pluck was sitting in the front room when Rafique entered the apartment. "Yo, where Eesh at?" Rafique asked, taking a seat on the sofa.

"She said she be right back. I think she went to the Chinese store."

"Alright. Look Pluck, I got two ounces for you. This me and you. I'ma leave this shit in your hands. If you want to just bag this shit up, sell it, and break down the money, we can do that. But if you want to stack this paper and keep flipping, we can do that, too. Whatever you decide to do, we just gonna go down the middle with it."

"Man, I'm trying to stack."

"Alright then, let's stack this paper. I had a feeling you would want to do it like this. I know I should've taken some more coke. We got like nine out that shit."

"Nine? Where the rest of it at?"

"I let Dre and Qua keep it. I took most of the money. Shit, two ain't enough?"

"Yeah, yeah, two cool."

The front door opening and closing ended their conversation.

"Hi, baby," Aisha said, walking through the front door with hands full of Chinese food.

"Hey, Eesh, what's wrong with you going to the store by yourself this time of night?"

"I wasn't by myself. Kenya, Cynthia, and Shay was with me. When Pluck came over, I knew you would be coming soon, so I went to get us something to eat."

"You see, that's why I love this girl, Pluck. She always got a motherfucker in mind. Eesh, I'm going in the bedroom. I'm tired, I'ma eat and go the fuck to sleep."

"Sleep? Sshhhiiittt, not if I can help it, at least not right away."

Rafique shook his head and headed to the bedroom with Aisha following right behind him.

The next morning, empty cartons of Chinese food littered the bedroom as the smell of cooking awakened Rafique. *Damn, why the fuck didn't Aisha pick this trash up?* Rafique got out the bed, gathered the trash up, and walked to the bathroom. Once he finished washing up, he walked into the kitchen. Aisha was cooking. Rafique quietly walked up behind her and hugged her tight. He placed a kiss on the nape of her neck. "That's for me, boo?"

"Yeah, I hope you like it. I made some cheese eggs, homefries, and some turkey bacon."

Aisha wasn't the best of cooks, and Rafique really wasn't looking forward to eating her breakfast. But on this morning, Aisha's cooking wasn't bad at all. After they finished eating, Rafique and Pluck thanked her for the food. Rafique planted a wet kiss on her mouth as he prepared to leave.

"Oh, so you just gonna eat and leave, huh?"

"Eesh, don't start that nagging shit. I'll see you later on." Rafique smiled, grabbed his keys, and left.

CHAPTER ELEVEN

Back at his motel room, it didn't take long for Rafique's thoughts to travel back to Philly and the woman he had left behind. *Damn, I been gone a week now and I haven't called her yet.* Rafique headed outside to the pay phone to call Tracey. He paused with the phone at his ear and his finger hovering, just about to press the ten digit number to his apartment. He didn't call Tracey. For some strange reason – to this day he still doesn't understand – instead of calling Tracey, he called his cousin Mike.

"Hello." Mike picked up after a couple rings.

"What's up, cuz?"

"Who this, Fique?"

"Yeah, it's me."

"Damn, what's up, man? Yo, I stopped by your crib last night to check up on your peoples. You know, to see if she needed anything. Man, some dude was leaving out as I was getting ready to ring the bell. The motherfucker was like, 'I'll call you later.' Fique, man, Tracey was like 'okay' and acted like that shit wasn't about nothing when she saw me standing there."

"What time was this?"

"It had to be like eleven, eleven thirty."

Rafique was hurt, but his ego didn't allow him to show it. He just played it off as if he didn't care. He talked to Mike for a few minutes more before making up an excuse to hang up. His head was pounding as he pushed the numbers to his apartment in Philly. *I can't believe this bitch.* The phone began to ring.

"Hello." Tracey picked up out of breath.

"Hey, what's up?"

"Rafique, before you say something, Mike stopped over here as a friend of mine was leaving the house. He had drove me home from work and had to use the bathroom. Your cousin saw him when he was leaving."

Deep down, Rafique knew she was lying, but he wanted to believe her, so he did. Tracey then turned the tables on him.

"So how come it took you so long to call me?"

"I've been busy. This was the first opportunity I had to call."

"Busy! Nigga, you mean to tell me that out of seven days you couldn't find a couple minutes to call me and let me know if you was safe."

At this point Rafique was hurt. His pain was an old pain that lovers throughout the centuries have felt after being betrayed. He didn't have the heart to argue, so he said nothing as Tracey continued to shout at him for twenty minutes before hanging up on him.

Rafique walked slowly back to his motel room. He lay in the bed and shut his eyes. The pain he was feeling was a familiar one, one that he hadn't felt since his daughter's mother's betrayal. It was a pain that he vowed to never experience again. But, here it was, just as devastating as it was the first time.

For the next few days, he stayed inside his motel room, only leaving out to eat. He just didn't want to be bothered by anyone. After a few days, though, he left out of his room. He realized that sitting in a dark room feeling sorry for himself would not make him feel any better. He had to get out, and, hopefully, time would heal his fractured heart.

Months had passed since that day. The summer months faded into the fall. During that time, he spent the majority of his time with Aisha, the best medicine for his ailing heart. She was good for him, almost making him forget about Tracey. But a couple months weren't enough time, and Rafique would soon find this out the hard way.

Pluck had, in a few short months, turned those two ounces into nine. So Rafique's finances were cool. Things were going pretty good for him. He had a woman that loved him and enough money to be okay. Things were going so well for him that he sometimes forgot that he was a wanted man. But like a sadist searching for their next source of pain, he called Tracey. It was the middle of the day on this bleak, cloudy, and chilly October afternoon. It was a weekday, so he had to call her at work.

"Pennsylvania Hospital. How can I help you?" It was Tracey. Her voice sent chills racing up and down his spine.

"Yeah, uhhh, Tracey?"

"Yeah, Rafique?"

"Yeah, it's me."

"Oh shit, boy! Where have you been? Why haven't you called me? I missed you so much."

"Tracey, I know you was lying to me the last time I talked to you. I mean, I feel like a real nut for even calling you now."

She started to protest, but Rafique cut her off.

"Tracey, the dude was leaving your house at eleven o'clock, you get off at eight. Look, it's cool, I know I put you in a fucked up situation, me being on the run and leaving you out there. I mean, you just might not be cut out for this kind of shit. But if that's what it is, then just be straight up with me-"

"Rafique, I'm sorry bab…"

Tracey stopped in the middle of her sentence. Rafique heard a scuffle over the phone. He then heard a man's voice shouting in the background. "Bitch, you ain't tell him yet?"

A man's voice spoke into the phone, "Hello."

Rafique's heart was pounding in his chest. "Yeah, what's up?"

"Why the fuck you keep calling my woman?"

"What the fuck you say?"

"Motherfucker, you heard me! I know she used to fuck with you, she told me all about you. But that's me now. Why you think she got that abortion?"

"What?"

"Oh, you ain't know about that, huh? Look, man, you playing yourself, stop calling my bitch."

A click and a dial tone was what Rafique heard next as he stood on the corner, mouth open in disbelief. Rafique slammed the phone down and raced to his room. He grabbed his car keys, his money, his gun, and in a heartbeat was speeding on 95 North.

Rafique got to Philly in a hour and a half. He went straight to Shawn's house. He had to stop there first because Tracey was at work and there were definitely too many cops at the hospital.

From the look on Rafique's face, Shawn could see that something was wrong. "Yo, Fique, what's up man? You back in town again, and you got this look on your face. What the fuck is up?"

"Man, I called Tracey at work."

Here we go with this bitch again.

"And some nigga got on the phone. Man, the motherfucker talked so greasy to me if I could've shot the motherfucker through the phone, I would've."

"What the nigga say?"

"He said all kind of shit. But the worse thing was when he said he made her get an abortion."

"Ssooo, okay, and."

"Okay, and? What the fuck you mean by that. You know what's next. I got to go see dude."

"You got to go see him?" Shawn could see the hurt and anger in his friend's face. He had to be delicate with this. He needed to get Rafique to think. "Fique, man, you know homicide be parked outside the apartment waiting for you to show up."

"Yeah, but Tracey said that they ain't been around in a while."

"Yo, come on, man is you serious? What the fuck is wrong with you? Who's to say that they won't be out there today? Are you willing to risk your life on that chance? Now say that they ain't out there and you see this nigga and you do something to him. Who's to say that rotten bitch won't tell on you? Come on, man, think. I know you're hurting, but you got to keep your emotions in check. Anytime you react like this you stop thinking. When you stop thinking you make bonehead mistakes."

Rafique was silent. He dropped his head. "You right, man. I'm tripping."

Shawn saved a man's life on that day. He won't be honored for doing a noble deed. No one will know, not even the man whom he saved; he'll just go on living, never knowing how close to death's door he came, or that a stranger saved his life.

Rafique never went back to DC. Why? He suffered from a bad case of youthful stupidity. How he could be comfortable in a city where he was a fugitive is a question for the ages. Maybe, because like most young men, he thought he could come up with a plan that was never thought of before, like staying at Shawn's house and only venturing out at night. Surely no one ever thought to do this before. As it turned out, someone had, and he would realize soon enough how bad a mistake it was for him to remain in Philly.

Two weeks had gone by and Rafique was living life by the day. He stuck to his routine: spending the daylight hours indoors, only venturing out in the evenings as if his dark skin could blend in with the nighttime, providing for him a natural camouflage. During this time, he began to get word that Tracey was calling around for him. She had called his mother, and she had called Shawn's house a couple times, just missing him. *I wonder what the fuck she calling around for me for.* A couple of days passed by before she caught him at Shawn's and his wondering came to an end. He had been sitting in the house waiting for the night when the phone rang. He picked up, "Hello."

"Rafique, is that you? It's me, Tracey. I've been calling all over for you. How have you been?"

"I been alright. What's up?"

"Dag, why you getting all like that?"

"Come on, man, what's up?"

"I miss you, that's what's up."

Rafique was silent for a moment, thinking, *What kind of game is this bitch playing. Fuck it, I'ma just play this thing out to see where it goes.*
"Rafique, you don't miss me?"
"Yeah, I mean, I miss you, but you ain't right. I heard you moved."
"Yeah, I moved. I had to leave our apartment. Too many bad memories."
"So what, you live with that dude now?"
"No, I live by myself."
Tracey paused for a moment. She looked at the phone as if she could see Rafique's face. "Let me stop lying to you. I live with him."
"You happy?"
"I'm okay, but I'd rather be with you."
"So where your man at now?"
"Oh, he in the other room getting on my nerves."
Rafique shook his head. *Damn, this a rotten bitch.* "Tracey, I'm trying to see you."
"For real? You ain't mad at me?"
"Naw, at least not no more."
"I want to see you so bad, baby. It's just so hard for me to get out. This motherfucker be smothering me. Soon as I get a chance, I'm coming to see you. I miss that dick."
Rafique couldn't take it anymore. "Hold the fuck up, man. If you miss me all like that, why the fuck you cross me?"
"Rafique, what if you go to jail? What was I supposed to do then? I had to do what was best for me and my son. This dude, he work, he ain't all out in the street. I have a stable home. I ain't got to worry about the police

knocking my door in. Oh shit, here he comes. I'ma call you back baby."

Tracey hung the phone up. Rafique sat there with the dial tone ringing in his ear. He smiled, *Damn, that's a selfish bitch. I kind of always knew she was like that. I just used to ignore that shit. Damn, I was a fucking nut.*

Rafique and Tracey would never renew their relationship. Although he talked to her a few more times, that part of his life had come to an end. Tracey had hurt him deeply, but he had no regrets. They shared some beautiful times together and she provided him with a life lesson that would be priceless. He was a wiser man because of this experience. Now if he could only stay out of jail, he would be able to put that experience to use.

CHAPTER TWELVE

For Rafique, being back in Philadelphia was like a recovering crack addict in a cocaine processing lab. There were just too many negative temptations. Before you knew it, he had slipped back into a very bad habit: drinking syrup and popping pills.

He was first exposed to these drugs as a teenager. At that time in his life, his sense of self-worth was at an all time low.

To be raised as a black child in America was like a foster child growing up in an abusive home. In the good ole U.S.A., Rafique had no positive reinforcement of his identity. Everything that was associated with the color he identified with culturally was systematically labeled as a negative. This, in turn, destroyed his self-esteem. So when he was introduced to a drug that made him feel good about himself, he was hooked. When he was high he didn't worry about being too black because the drug influenced him not to care. To Rafique's young impressionable mind, to be high was to be at the top of his game. It lowered his inhibitions; if there was a girl he wanted to talk to, he stepped right to her. His insecurities temporarily vanished. Being high also had its drawbacks, but Rafique hated himself so much that the drawbacks didn't even register. He believed that his judgments were sound, even when they weren't. You would think that being wanted for a murder that you couldn't remember committing would have been enough for Rafique to leave drugs alone forever. It was, for a brief period of time. It was just that being back in Philadelphia, and the paranoia of being a fugitive, pushed him right back to the thing that had him running in the first place.

His father kept leaving messages with his mother, pleading for Rafique to return to DC, but he never returned his father's calls. Shawn kept telling him to go back, but he ignored Shawn. Aisha couldn't convince him to return either. Rafique would promise her he was coming back, but then he would get high and all of his promises would be forgotten.

So on June 6, 1992 – a year and a month since the first day he discovered the police were looking for him – he was arrested.

It happened on a hot and humid summer night as Rafique and four of his friends were sitting on the fence that surrounded Malcolm X Park. He had just drunk some syrup and took ten Valiums. As the effects of the drugs began to hit him, everything slowed down. Rafique was seeing things in slow-motion as the weed was being passed back and forth between him and a few of his friends. Rafique could see the police car as it approached, but he was high and felt no threat.

"Yo, get rid of the weed," his friend Cloud said.

A lone police officer got out the van and walked towards them. The cop's hand was poised over the .45 automatic that was in its holster.

"Everybody, up against the car!"

The five friends did as they were told. They each got off the fence and walked to the curb where they lined up putting their hands on the hood of a car that was parked in front of them. The young white cop nervously approached and began searching them one by one. After he was done, Rafique could hear the clicking of the handcuffs as the cop cuffed one of his friends.

"Yo, man, what the fuck you locking me up for?" Rafique's friend said, looking over his shoulder as the cop grabbed the cuffs tightly and directed him to the police van.

"You're under investigation for a homicide," the cop answered as he opened the back doors of the police van, putting Rafique's friend inside.

Once the cop said those words, Rafique's heart rate quickened, but he remained calm. After being on the run for a year, he understood that the uniformed cops really didn't know who he was. It was the homicide detectives who handled his case that caused him worry. After five minutes had passed, the cop called for backup and said, "Okay, you guys can take your hands down. As a matter of fact, y'all can leave."

Rafique and his friends began to walk away. At that very same instant about ten cop cars pulled up. The backup had arrived. They began jumping out of their cars, heading straight towards the young men.

Rafique kept his cool, partly because he was high. Rafique kept walking. *If I get out of this shit here, I'm outta here and I ain't ever coming back.* Rafique was almost clear when a cop grabbed him from behind. "O'brien, let's take this one, too. Hold up, take those dark ass glasses off."

Rafique removed his glasses and looked the cop in the eyes.

"Okay, let that other guy go and take this one."

Handcuffed now in the back of the police van, Rafique felt like the biggest fool in the world. His self-pity didn't last long, though. With the excitement of the arrest wearing off, the adrenaline coursing through his body began to subside, allowing the narcotics he took to regain its hold as he nodded off.

Fifteen minutes later, light flooded the back of the van as the doors opened, waking Rafique up.

"Okay, murderer, you're home now. Let's go," the young white police officer said, standing by the open doors waiting for Rafique to get up.

Rafique was in a drug-induced haze and he moved as if he was walking under water. He stepped down out the van, looked at his surrounding and recognized immediately where he was at. The Roundhouse – also known as the Police Administration Building. Rafique walked to the front desk where they removed his handcuffs and told him to empty his pockets and remove his belt and shoestrings. Once Rafique complied, they escorted him to the bubble.

The bubble was a holding pen that was always overcrowded. A room that was designed to accommodate fifteen or twenty men at the most always held at least fifty to sixty men, with the weekend being the most crowded. Of course, this had to be the weekend as Rafique entered the cell.

His nostrils were assaulted immediately by the foul odor of at least forty men passing gas, day-old vomit, cigarette smoke, and alcohol that oozed from the pores and mouths of the drunken men that lay sprawled all over the floor and benches. Rafique held his breath and looked at the back wall. Welded into that back wall were four phones. This is where Rafique headed. Gingerly, he navigated his way through all the drunks and reached the phones. He picked up the receiver, and the first person he called was his mother.

"Hello," Tonya picked up the phone her voice heavy with sleep.

"Hey, Mom, it's me. I was just calling you to let you know that they got me. I'm locked up."

Tonya initially sounded relieved. She no longer had to worry about the police shooting her boy down like a dog like they were threatening to do. After the initial relief, the realization of his predicament set in. "Rafique, why did you come back?"

Rafique couldn't answer that question. Instead, he just said, "Look, Mom, I don't know how this situation is gonna turn out. Pray for me, okay?"

"Of course, baby, I'll pray for you. Are you okay?"

"Yeah, I'm cool. I love you Mom."

"I love you, too, Rafique."

They talked for a few minutes more before Rafique hung up and called another number.

"Hello." Aisha picked up the phone and her voice was thick with sleep as well.

"Hey, boo."

At hearing Rafique's voice, Aisha became fully awake. "Rafique, is that you? Where are you?"

"I'm locked up. Eesh, I got some things that I need to tell you, so listen for a minute before you say anything."

With the drugs wreaking havoc throughout his body, his voice began to slur again. Aisha recognized this. "Rafique, what's wrong with you? Why you sound like that?"

"Nothing man, damn. Would you listen for a minute? The reason why I came out there so suddenly was because I was on the run for a homicide. That's also why I wouldn't stay at your house. I didn't want the police finding me there and kicking your door in. I didn't want to take you through all that."

Aisha was silent for a moment, processing what he said. "Rafique, Rafique!"

Rafique had nodded off while waiting for her to respond. "Huh, what's up?"

This motherfucker drunk or something. I can hear it all in his voice. "Look, baby, I'll be out there on the first train tomorrow, just give me you–"

Rafique cut her off mid-sentence and said the hardest thing he had ever said up to this point in his life. "Don't come out here, I'm cool. Eesh, you got your whole life ahead of you. You still young, you look good as a motherfucker. Baby, I don't know how this shit gonna turn out. Ain't no telling when I'm coming home. So what I want you to do is live your life. Forget about me. If I beat this case, I'ma be on the first thing smoking out there. If not, you probably won't hear from me again. I can't let you do this bid with me. It wouldn't be fair to you."

Aisha was crying by the time he finished talking. Through the sobs, she responded, "Rafique, why don't you wait till you sober before you make a decision like this. Furthermore, you can't tell me how to live my life. That has to be my decisi…"

Before she could finish, Rafique hung up the phone. He didn't want to give her a chance to influence him to change his mind.

Rafique began dialing numbers again. The next person he called was Shawn. Shawn picked up right away as if he was waiting for Rafique to call. "Hello."

"Shawn, what's up? It's me."

"Goddamn, man, you high as a motherfucker. Yo, look, I've been waiting for you to call. Fique, you know how you got locked up?"

"Man, what the fuck is that, a trick question?"

"Listen, man, the nigga that told on you, Fuzz, well his little brother was in the back seat of one of them police cars. The little nigga pointed you out to the police."

Rafique was fighting off the urge to nod again as he thought about what Shawn said. Things began to make sense. Now he understood why the police grabbed him from behind. What he couldn't understand was why would Fuzz's little brother point him out to the police.

After talking to Shawn for a few more minutes, he hung up the phone, leaned against the wall, and nodded off again.

"Rafique Johnson!"

His name being called snapped him out of his nod. It was time to be fingerprinted and photographed. After that was done, he was brought back to the bubble just in time for the cold egg sandwich and juice. Rafique had no appetite, so he gave his meal away and nodded off once more.

"Fuck y'all punk motherfuckers!"

Rafique was startled out of his nod. He looked up to see a young black man penned up against the fiberglass wall of the bubble. Two burly white cops were restraining him. After they had him subdued, they half dragged, half carried him to the back where there were smaller holding cells. As Rafique began to nod off again, he heard an ear-piercing scream. "AAAAAHHHHHHH! Please take these cuffs off. I can't feel my hands!"

Rafique recognized that voice. It was the same young man who had been dragged to the back. By cuffing his hands extra tight, the blood circulation to his hands was cut off, causing them to go numb. This was their sadistic way of teaching him a lesson. Rafique shook his head and nodded off again.

After a long night of nodding and being processed into the system, they finally called Rafique to see the judge about bail. Rafique and about six other prisoners were led up a flight of stairs to the Roundhouse's courtroom. They were placed in a holding cell to await the judge.

"Rafique Johnson." He didn't have to wait long for the bailiff to call his name. It was time to see the judge. To Rafique, this part of the process was a waste of time. He already knew that he would be either denied a bail or the bail would be so high it would be like he didn't have one. A sheriff escorted him from the holding cell to stand in front of the judge. Rafique looked up at the judge sitting on his throne-like bench shuffling papers while waiting on the judge to address him.

"Mr. Johnson, you've been charged with a general charge of murder, robbery, conspiracy, violation of the firearms act, and possession of an instrument of crime. It also says here that you were a fugitive for over a year. Taking all this into consideration, it's been determined by this court that you would be a flight risk. Bail denied!"

The judge slammed his gavel and Rafique was ushered back into the holding cell. It was very quiet when he took his seat. Most of the young men he was in the cell with were getting bails and eventually going home. When they overheard the seriousness of Rafique's situation, a solemn mood was placed over the cell. An hour later, after all the other prisoners had seen the judge, Rafique was returned to the bubble to await the trip to the county jail.

"CHOW!"

It was time to eat at the Burg, and the call to chow snapped Rafique out of his memories.

CHAPTER THIRTEEN

MAY 1991

"Yo, you a fucking nut! Damn," Lisa shouted into the phone. "Why you keep calling me? I told you I don't want you no more. What's wrong with you? Why can't you understand that?"

"Damn, Lisa, what I do?"

Lisa chuckled, "You see, that's just it, it ain't about nothing you did or didn't do. I just don't want your motherfucking ass no more. But no, you just got to keep on playing yourself. Look, Fuzz, just stop the fuck calling me, please!"

CLICK!

Fuzz was shocked and hurt as he stared into the phone in disbelief. Lisa had been his girl for the past two years, when all of a sudden she started acting funny. When Fuzz confronted her about it, she initially acted as if he was just being insecure, but after a while the acting stopped, and she just cut him off. This was what that phone call was just about. *Fuck that bitch. All these bitches out here, I can't believe I'm acting like this about this bitch.*

As Fuzz was thinking to himself, the doorbell rang. Fuzz rubbed his hands through his curly hair and got up to answer the door. "Who is it?"

"It's me, nigga." It was Tyrique, his current friend. Fuzz greeted him with a handshake and a quick embrace when he opened the door.

"What's up, Rique?"

"What's up, Fuzz?" Tyrique responded, following Fuzz back into his house.

"It's time to party, dog. I got that paper."

"Oh, yeah? When you settle the case?"

"A couple days ago. My lawyer called me today and told me to come sign the check. So what you wanna do?"

"Whatever, nigga, I'm with you."

For the next few days, Tyrique and Fuzz splurged: shopping, partying, and getting high. Tyrique really looked out for his main man Fuzz. The two of them had been friends since the fifth grade, and Tyrique had a genuine love for him. There was no question in his mind that if the shoe were on the other foot, Fuzz would've done the same thing for him.

A few days later at Tyrique's house, Fuzz and Chantel, Tyrique's girl, were sitting in the front room watching TV. Fuzz peered through the dimly-lit room, his eyes focused on Chantel. Her ebony skin seemed to sparkle as the light from the TV reflected off her face.

Something on TV made her smile as she flashed a set of perfect pearly-white teeth.

This bitch is a cold-blooded freak and this nigga Rique don't even know it. Fuzz licked his lips and began rubbing himself. He checked his watch. *Rique just left, he ain't gonna be back for about an hour, if that.* "Chantel, come here."

"Uh-uh. No, Fuzz. What if Tyrique come back?"

"Girl, get over here! He just left. Plus, he went all the way down North Philly. We got time."

Chantel got up and moved slowly to the couch where Fuzz was seated and she sat on his lap. Fuzz immediately started kissing her in the mouth. He then moved to her neck as he fondled her breast. She moaned as Fuzz's hands traveled from her breast to her ample backside. Chantel's breathing became rapid as Fuzz's hands roamed under her skirt, squeezing her ass.

"Ohhh yyyeeesss. Wait a minute, baby." Chantel got up, removed her panties, and bent over the arm of the couch.

Fuzz didn't hesitate. He got up, dropped his pants, and pulled his underwear down to his ankles and entered her from the back.

"Ooooh yes, Fuzz, I like it when you do me like this. Fuck me, baby, yyyeesss."

Sweat dripped from his head and landed on her back as Fuzz pushed hard, fast, and deep. Ten minutes later it was over. No words were spoken as Chantel stood up and went upstairs to the bathroom. Fuzz pulled his pants back up. He smiled. *Damn, I'm fucking my man's girl. Fuck it, that pussy too good to be having a conscious.*

Twenty minutes later, Tyrique came through the door, totally unaware of the betrayal that took place in his home. "I got it, homes, three and a half ounces. That should be cool, right?"

"Yeah, uh, look Rique, I got to make a run. I'll be back a little later on."

Fuzz left and went home. When he got inside, he went straight to the phone and called a guy named Roach that he dealt with sometimes. After a few rings, a male's voice answered the phone.

✲ ✲ ✲

The marijuana smoke drifted lazily upwards, leaving dancing shadows on the walls, as Roach sat on his bed in the basement of his mother's home smoking a joint.

The basement was aglow in the eerie red light, giving the newly renovated basement a look of an early 1970's apartment. Glow-in-the-dark posters of Bruce Lee decorated the walls. A heavy drumbeat vibrated in Roach's ears as he nodded his head to the rap song that was blasting from the twelve-inch woofers he had placed strategically around the room. This was his chill time. He reached over to pluck the ashes from the joint into the ashtray. The weed had him overanalyzing the sounds. It seemed as if his senses were amplified as he noticed sounds that he ordinarily wouldn't have paid attention to. The marijuana and music had him in a zone. Roach smiled as his mind began to reflect on his life and how much he had changed over the last few years.

From his earliest days, Roach could remember when he was just like any other young boy growing up in the mean streets of North Philly. He was just a little different, though. Roach was a momma's boy, spoiled rotten.

Roach's mother, Alicia, gave birth to him when she was but a child herself at fourteen. Although she was a child, she loved her son deeply, and she took very good care of him. With the help of her mother, who was a young mother herself at thirty, Alicia was able to provide for her son all the things that people define themselves by. Alicia was a very materialistic girl. Being mature for her young age, Alicia had an understanding about life that most girls her age didn't have.

Roach's father, Bryant, was an older, married man who had a thing for young girls. With a family of his own, he did a lot of creeping – finding young vulnerable girls, exploiting their naivety, using them up, and then discarding them. He was a predator on the hunt for fresh meat, and a young fatherless Alicia didn't stand a chance.

Like a hawk spotting a rabbit, Bryant saw Alicia walking home from school. He pulled up in his new 1972 Cadillac Seville and began the game of seduction. Alicia didn't feel apprehensive because Bryant had a baby face. Alicia just assumed that he was one of the many young hustlers who were always coming at her. His young face fooled may young girls, and just like all the ones before her, Alicia would make the same mistake.

After that first day she was hooked. Bryant schooled her to a lot of things, but the one thing that would serve her well in the years to come was when he taught her how to use her physical assets to her advantage. Bryant blew her mind sexually. After all, she was a fourteen-year-old girl with little sexual experience. Alicia was hopelessly in love. This was the reason why she never pressed him about where he lived or why she couldn't have his phone number. The one time she asked him, he snapped, and Alicia couldn't bear to have Bryant upset with her. He kept her so off balance that she began to believe it was wrong for her to even think of those things.

After about eight months Alicia became pregnant. She told him immediately and that was the last time she saw him. Alicia was crushed when he stopped coming around. She tried everything she could to find him, but all she knew was his first name, which wasn't very much to go on. Eventually, with the help of her mother, she was able to move on and get through her pregnancy.

Nine months later she gave birth to a beautiful baby boy that she named Steven, after her mother's father. Little Steve got his nickname Roach when he was a toddler. Steve liked to walk around barefoot and step on roaches.

As a result of this life experience, along with the advice of Bryant, Alicia took advantage of the young hustlers. This was how she was able to provide for herself as well as her son.

Growing up, Roach never wanted for nothing. As he got older, this caused the other young men in the neighborhood to become jealous. Roach had all the young girls, the fly clothes, and the money. Every time something new came out, Roach had it. When you live in a world of have-nots and you have, it's inevitable that envy will raise its ugly head.

It all culminated one day as he stood on the corner, drinking forties with a couple of his friends. They were so absorbed in their conversation that they didn't notice the car with the tinted windows slowly pulling up beside them until it was too late. A hail of automatic gunfire rained down upon them like a hailstorm. One of Roach's friends lay motionless with a bullet wound to the head, and Roach lay right next to him, critically wounded and clinging to life by a thread.

Because of his youth, Roach was able to recover physically after spending months recuperating in the hospital. While at the hospital, he had to see a psychologist who determined that Roach would need psychotherapy. But after Roach healed physically he left the hospital, never taking the psychologist's advice, leaving the psychological scars still bleeding.

Home now, the first thing Roach did was purchase a gun. You see, his attitude was one of shoot first or be shot. He promised himself that he would never be in a position of weakness again. Roach decided he would be the aggressor. If someone had a problem with him, they would think twice before confronting him, because if they did and they weren't successful, there would be a heavy price to pay.

After a couple of years and numerous shootings and armed robberies, Roach had achieved the image he so desperately sought. He wasn't a momma's boy any longer, and no one dared called him that again.

Roach smiled again as he recalled these events, exposing his gold front tooth that contrasted with his very dark skin tone. The phone rang, bringing Roach back to the present. He picked it up. "Hello."

✯ ✯ ✯

The phone rang in Fuzz's ear a couple times before Roach answered. "Hello."

"Yo, Roach, what's up?"

"Who this?"

"It's Fuzz."

"Oh, what's up?"

"Look, man, I know this nigga out here. He got like eight stacks and three and a half ounces. The nigga sweet. He ain't got no hammer or nothing. I'm telling you man, this'll be the easiest couple dollars you'll make in a while."

"When you want to do this?"

"Tomorrow."

"Alright, call me when you ready."

The next day, Roach arrived at Fuzz's house. He got Tyrique's address and Fuzz informed him where Tyrique kept all the money and drugs. Armed with all the information he needed, Roach left.

The rain fell in a misty haze as Roach pulled up in front of Tyrique's house. Roach found a parking spot and walked up to the front door of the row home. Roach rang the bell. Adrenaline pumped through his veins, preparing Roach for the robbery. Seconds ticked past and then the door opened. "What's up?" Tyrique stood in the doorway to his home, a puzzled expression etched across his face.

"Is Stephanie home?"

"Don't no Stephanie live here."

"Damn, I can't believe this bitch gave me the wrong address." Roach said as he turned his back to Tyrique.

Tyrique smiled. He knew all too well what he believed Roach was feeling. He was always getting wrong addresses and phone numbers. "Naw, homes, she don't live here, and I know for a fact don't nobody on this block go by that name." Tyrique thought he was being helpful.

"Damn, my fault." Roach turned back around to face Tyrique, but instead of being thankful, he had a 9mm in his hand. "Nigga, turn around and get the fuck back in the house!"

Tyrique's heart slammed against his chest cavity as he stared down the barrel of the gun. He was exposed with no way out, so he did what he was told. He heard the door shut behind him and felt the gun in his back. A voice then intimately close, whispered into his ear.

"Okay, where the fuck is the money and coke at?"

"What?"

"You heard me, motherfucker!"

As Roach spoke these words, he raised the gun in the air. He was about to add a little pain for some incentive.

Out the corner of his eye, Tyrique saw Roach raise the gun and panic set in, he ran. To run was a fatal mistake.

The loud retort of the 9mm shook the walls of the house as Roach squeezed the trigger. The bullet slammed into Tyrique's back, sending him crashing to the floor. Tyrique lost consciousness. Roach stepped over Tyrique and looked down. "You stupid motherfucker, you should've just taken the lump. Now look at you." Roach kicked Tyrique in the ribs. He already knew where the money was, so he headed upstairs to retrieve it.

Forty-five minutes later, Roach was relaxing in Fuzz's house. Marijuana smoke filled the air of Fuzz's room as Roach ran down the story.

"Why would that stupid motherfucker run? Silly ass nigga. You get all the money?"

Roach smiled and pulled out $7,500 and the drugs. Roach counted out $2,000 and grabbed an ounce of cocaine. He handed it to Fuzz. "Man, that shit was sweet. Next time you run across a vic like this, make sure you call me first."

"Don't I always?"

Roach stubbed the joint out in the ashtray, got up, shook Fuzz's hand, and left. Alone now, Fuzz emptied his ounce of cocaine out and began to chop it up.

Two hours later as he lay on his bed watching TV, the phone rang. "Hello."

A female's voice crying hysterically into the phone rattled his eardrum. "Fuzz, they, they, shot Ty-Tyrique!!"

"Hold the fuck up! Who this?"

"I-i-it's Chantel."

"Hold up, calm the fuck down! Now tell me what happened."

Chantel paused in an effort to get herself together. Then she spoke, this time more clearly, "Tyrique's been shot. I'm at the hospital now. He's been shot in the back. I don't know if he's going to make it."

"What hospital you at?"

"I'm at Penn."

"I'll be right there." Fuzz hung up the phone, irritated because he had to drive all the way to the hospital.

Fuzz arrived at the hospital and spotted Chantel as soon as he walked in. She was still crying. He walked up to her, and she walked into his arms.

"Chantel, what happened?" he stated, holding her tight.

" I don't know. All I know is when I got to his house earlier, the door was open. I walked in and found him lying in a pool of blood."

"Did you find out how he was doing?"

"Yeah, the doctor just left. He said that he would live, but he may never walk again."

Fuzz shook his head and pounded his fist into the wall. If the Academy Award for best ghetto actor was given out at the end of the year, Fuzz would win it hands down. Fuzz could care less about Tyrique getting shot; after all, it was to his benefit. All Fuzz cared about at that moment was what his body was feeling for Chantel. "Where he at?" Fuzz asked.

"He's in intensive care."

"I'm going to see him."

"Fuzz, you can't go see him right now. Only family."

Fuzz acted as if he couldn't hear Chantel. He kept walking until he came upon a men's restroom. He stopped and the fake tears began to roll down his cheeks. Chantel saw the fake tears. The tears pulled at the strings of her heart, causing her to walk up to Fuzz and embrace him. Fuzz just held her at first, but after a few seconds, his lips found her neck. He sucked lightly and his hands roamed up and down her backside. Fuzz began backing into the restroom. He kept backing up until he reached the last stall. He reached back, found the door handle, and opened the door. He stepped in, stopped, and turned her around. Fuzz closed the door behind him. He embraced her again.

"Fuzz, this ain't right, and it stinks in here."

"Chantel, I need you right now, I need you bad."

Fuzz began to kiss again. Slowly, he moved from her lips to her neck, and then to her earlobe. His hands, at the same time, eased under her white tennis skirt.

"Fuzz, no, please stop," Chantel moaned.

Fuzz kept going, though. His hands found her hot spot and began to gently rub. What little resistance Chantel had, melted away.

Fuzz wasn't always like this, but circumstance, environment, and negative influence shaped the character of the man he had grown up to be.

He was raised in his maternal grandmother's home, along with seven uncles, in abject poverty. They lived in a vermin-infested house that had no food most of the time. Fuzz, at a very tender age, learned how to fend for himself. In doing so, he developed a very self-centered personality.

Fuzz's uncles thought that by showing him no love, Fuzz would grow up to be tough. So in a warped way, they believed that by abusing him they were showing him their love.

Fuzz was ridiculed badly by the other children. "Dirty Fuzz" was what they called him. They teased him about his hand-me-down clothing, his holey sneakers, and his poor hygiene. As a result of this, Fuzz was a loner. The older he got the more he embraced his role. These negative influences turned him into a very cold-hearted person. Fuzz only cared about himself. He studied the lessons of his uncles and he learned how to take care of himself by any means necessary. To show love, compassion, or loyalty were things to be looked upon as traits of weakness. He also learned how to be a master of deceit. Fuzz masked his selfishness. He developed false friendships that would only be used for his benefit. So he had no real friends. Even with Lisa – although he told himself he loved her – the reality was he didn't know how to love. Lisa was just convenient for him. He just couldn't stand the fact that she might be with someone else.

After Fuzz left the hospital, he went back home. He began to worry about if Tyrique could connect him to the robbery. Fuzz was the only person, besides Chantel, who knew Tyrique had a little cocaine and some money. After a few minutes, though, he calmed down as he began to reassure himself. *Fuck it, what can he do if he do put it together? Not a motherfucking thing. The nigga need to be worried about learning how to walk again.*

Later on that evening, Fuzz sat at the bar of the neighborhood after-hour spot. Fuzz was sipping on his favorite drink, sloe gin and orange juice, as he searched the crowd for a potential one-night stand. The music trekked though his body, sending waves of vibration, pulsating, pounding, forcing his body to involuntarily move in time with the beat. *What the fuck! Is that Lisa over there with that nigga?* Fuzz squinted his eyes for a clearer look. *It damn sure is. That bitch!* In a corner booth, Lisa and Rafique were sitting down enjoying each other's company. As Fuzz watched, Lisa began kissing Rafique on his face and neck. Fuzz was angry. *That's why that bitch been acting all funny. She must be fucking that nigga now.* As these thoughts raced through his mind, Lisa and Rafique stood up and walked to the dance floor. At the same time, the tempo of the music changed as a slow guitar rift filled the club. During the guitar intro, Sadiq, of the band Toni Toney Tony, effortlessly blended his second-tenor voice perfectly with the peak of the guitar solo.

I DON'T WISH YOU NO BAD LUCK BABY,
I DON'T WISH YOU PAIN,
I ONLY WANT TO EXPOSE YOUR LIFE TO THE
FINER THIIINGGSS......

As the hit "Whatever You Want" flowed from the speakers, Rafique and Lisa slowly danced, holding each other as if they were the last two people on the planet. To Fuzz, this was the ultimate humiliation, as his girl lovingly accepted Rafique feeling all over her body as everyone watched. Fuzz thought about stepping to them but then thought better of it. *Naw. If I do that, niggas gonna be saying I went out like a nut about a bitch.* So Fuzz did nothing but watch.

After a while, Rafique and Lisa left the club. Fuzz wanted to follow them but decided against it. He just sat back with the music. The pounding faded from his ears as he focused on how to get Rafique out of the way. He wanted his girl back.

CHAPTER FOURTEEN

The clickety-clack of the dice rattling in Fuzz's hand came to a stop as he flung the dice against the wall. His anxiety level rose as he watched the dice twirl around on the ground for a few seconds before resting on the five and two-craps.

"Shit, today ain't my day. I can't even hit a fucking six," Fuzz mumbled.

"What you say, son? You done? Or you gonna give me some more of that paper," said Righteous, a dude from New York who sold cocaine down the street from Fuzz's grandmother's house. "Give me those dice, son. You ain't shaking them right." Righteous dropped a hundred-dollar bill on the ground, grabbed the dice from Fuzz's outstretched hand and shook them. Righteous tossed the dice and watched in anticipation as they landed on two fours. "Eight, nigga! Bet a nickel."

Fuzz counted out six hundred and laid it on the ground. If Righteous hit this number, Fuzz would be broke.

Righteous shook the dice again. He slung the dice against the wall. He snapped his fingers just as the dice left his hand. The dice landed and started spinning.

Before they came to a complete halt, Fuzz stepped on them. "Give me them."

"Damn son, you scared? A scared man can't win," Righteous said as he picked up the dice, shook them again and slung them against the wall. The dice bounced to a stop on five and three. "Eight, nigga! Move so I can get my money. What? Damn, son, you broke? I know you ain't broke. Dig deep and drop some more money on the ground."

Fuzz didn't respond. He just turned and walked away angry.

Righteous didn't help matters as he yelled at Fuzz's back. "Go get some more paper son. I ain't going nowhere. I'll be here when you get back."

Fuzz was angry but he kept walking without saying anything or looking back. You see, Fuzz already had it in his mind that Righteous was getting robbed.

An hour later, Fuzz turned the corner of Delancey Street and walked up to the house Righteous hustled out of. Righteous was sitting on the porch. Fuzz stopped and began walking up the steps.

"Okay son, I see you back to give me some more of that paper."

"Naw man, I'm done. I just came back to holla at Busta." Busta owned the house and allowed Righteous to sell cocaine out of it. This way he could smoke for free. Fuzz walked past Righteous and entered the dark house. Fuzz headed straight up the stairs and walked to the back room where Busta usually held court. Fuzz knocked on the door and waited patiently for someone to answer.

"Who is it?" a hoarse voice said from behind the door.

"It's me, Fuzz."

"Come on in."

Fuzz entered the bedroom, stepping on empty crack vials as his nose was assaulted by the smell of a mixture of burning cocaine, matches, and incense. Fuzz looked around. *Damn, this motherfucker filthy.* Clothes were tossed haphazardly everywhere. Plates with half-eaten and rotten food littered the room. Busta was sitting on a piss-stained mattress with no sheets that was sitting on crates. He held a glass pipe to his ashy, white lips and pulled on it heavily. Bernadette was sitting next to him with her eyes as wide as dinner plates, glued to the pipe. A musty odor that came from her mingled with all the other foul smells and drifted up to Fuzz's nose. He stepped away from her to avoid the stench. "Ay, Busta, I need to holla at you a minute."

"Okay, young buck. Bernadette, step outside for a minute so I can holla at my young buck." Bernadette reluctantly got up. She didn't want to leave the room. If she did, that would mean less cocaine for her to smoke. She sucked her teeth and rolled her eyes at Fuzz. Fuzz paid her no mind and began to talk as soon as she left the room. "Look, Busta, if it's cool with you, I'ma get that nigga Righteous robbed."

Busta stood up. His eyes fixed on a spot on the floor. Busta bent over suddenly and picked up a piece of lint. He flicked the lint back to the floor; it wasn't a piece of coke like he thought it was. He scanned the floor some more as he answered Fuzz. "I don't give a fuck what you do. As long as I get a breakdown."

As the two of them continued to talk, they both were unaware that Bernadette stood outside the cracked door and heard everything that was said.

"Alright, Busta, I'm out man."

Fuzz turned and left out the room and almost knocked Bernadette down. "Damn, bitch, he ain't gonna smoke all the fucking coke. Get the fuck out the damn way."

"Fuck you, Fuzz!"

Fuzz didn't respond as he hurriedly left out the house. As soon as he stepped outside, Fuzz took a deep breath to clear his nostrils of the awful odors of the crackhouse. He exhaled and took the short walk down the street to his grandmother's house. Fuzz sat in his room and lit up a cigarette. *Yeah, I'ma get this nigga and I know just who to call.* Fuzz picked up the phone and began dialing numbers.

"Speak." Roach picked up the phone on the first ring.

"Roach, this Fuzz. I got something sweet for you, homie."

"Oh yeah? What's up?"

"This nut-ass nigga from New York be selling coke out this house down the street from me. I know he got at least five stacks on him. He pulled out his money and was talking shit when we was shooting dice. The house be doing nice numbers, and he told me they be flipping like nine and a half. I don't know where the stash at, though. I know he be keeping money in his sock. All you got to do is clunk the nigga in the head a couple times and he'll tell you where the rest of that bread at."

"Is he strapped?"

"Naw, the nigga ain't strapped. Didn't I tell you it was something sweet?"

"Alright. So when you want to do this?"

"Meet me on the corner of 52nd & Delancy Street at quarter to ten."

Later on that evening, Fuzz headed to the corner of 52nd & Delancey Street. When he arrived, Chisel Head

Mike was sitting in his car with Rakim's "Move The Crowd" blasting from the car's sound system. Rafique, Buff, Tashi, and Ab were already there. *There go that nigga Rafique, This nut-ass nigga all high. I should fuck him up.* Fuzz didn't act on this thought because the rest of the guys would have intervened. So instead he waited, Rafique was always high. He knew he would have another opportunity and wouldn't have to wait long. "What's up? Y'all want to get some money?"

All four men declined, so Fuzz struck up a conversation while he waited for Roach to show up. Fifteen minutes would tick by before Roach arrived. Fuzz left without a word and walked towards Roach's car. By the time he reached the car, Roach was getting out.

"You ready to get this money?" Fuzz asked.

"Yeah, nigga, let's go."

Fuzz and Roach started walking towards 54th and Delancey Streets. Once they arrived at Busta's house, Fuzz pointed it out and said, "There go the house right there. Look, I'm parked down the street on Spruce. I'ma be there waiting on you."

"Alright, homie, let me go get this paper."

The two of them split up, Roach to Busta's house and Fuzz to his car.

Roach slowly approached the house. Once again he got a surge of adrenaline as he walked up the steps. Roach knocked lightly on the door. Righteous opened the door immediately. "What's up? What you need?"

"Let me get ten," Roach responded.

Righteous reached in his pocket and pulled out a ziplock bag full of crack vials. When he looked up after counting out ten, he was staring down the barrel of a gun. Seeing the chrome-plated 45-caliber pistol and Roach's hand steady on the trigger, Righteous swallowed hard. He knew the laws of the street so he complied. Righteous backed up into the house and proceeded to empty out his pockets. Righteous handed the drugs and money to Roach.

Roach glared at Righteous. "Nigga, give me that money you got in your sock. You think this shit a game? I know you got more paper on you."

As Roach was talking, he broke the number one rule of stickups: never take your eye off the vic. Roach only transgressed this unwritten law for a second, but that was all the time Righteous needed as he lunged for the gun. Roach saw Righteous make his move and fired one shot, hitting Righteous in the chest. Righteous fell to the floor, and Roach immediately went for his socks, taking everything he could find.

Once he was gone, Bernadette came out of the living room. She was the reason Roach had taken his eye off Righteous. He saw her out the corner of his eye as she ducked behind a chair. Bernadette walked over to where Righteous had lain. She sat on the floor and cradled his head in her lap. Bernadette liked Righteous. He had a good heart, or at least in her eyes he did. Righteous was the only crack dealer she knew that would just give her free cocaine. "Righteous, hold on. Everything's gonna be okay."

Blood began oozing from Righteous mouth and he started wheezing as his lungs filled with fluid. Righteous took his last breath, far from home, in a strange city, and in the arms of a stranger.

Meanwhile, Roach had made it to Fuzz's car.

"I heard a gunshot, what happened?" Fuzz asked as Roach got in the car and shut the door.

"Nigga, you asking a lot of questions."

Fuzz didn't respond. He didn't want to get on Roach's bad side because he knew Roach wouldn't hesitate to kill him. Fuzz pulled off and kept silent. *If he want me to know what happened, he'll tell me when he ready.* Not too long after that, the two of them sat in Fuzz's room. Roach pulled out fifteen hundred in cash and a thousand in coke.

"Man, that shit wasn't as sweet as you said. I had to shoot that motherfucker. That nut-ass nigga tried to grab the gun. I ain't get a chance to get the stash. All I got is this punk-ass couple dollars and this coke. Everything was cool until the motherfucker tried to take the gun. I had to down him then." Roach failed to mention the money he took out of Righteous' sock. "Look, man, you take this coke and I'll keep this punk-ass couple dollars. You know I ain't no coke selling motherfucker no way. I still got coke left from the last thing we did. Yo, dude might not make it. I hit him point blank in the chest."

"Man, I don't give a fuck, as long as we got something out of this shit."

As Fuzz and Roach were having this conversation, the police, in the meantime, had arrived at the scene of the shooting. After interviewing all the people in the house and getting no leads, the last person they interviewed was Bernadette.

"I don't know who the shooter was, but I know the guy who set him up to get robbed."

The detective who was interviewing her paused from taking notes, "Are you sure?"

"Yeah, I'm sure. I was in Busta's house and I overheard Fuzz ask if it was cool to get Righteous robbed. Busta told him he ain't give a fuck." With that statement, Bernadette had just sealed Fuzz's fate.

CHAPTER FIFTEEN

It was the early morning hours just before the sun peeked above the horizon. No sounds could be heard, and there was no movement on this quiet block. It was like a snapshot out of a moment in time. Suddenly, there was a hand signal. The police poised outside Fuzz's front and back door had been waiting on this signal to kick in the doors of the row home. Abrupt motion and the crashing in of the doors were followed by loud shouts. "Police! Hands up! Don't fucking move!"

Fuzz was asleep. The loud crash and the shouts awakened him. He was unnerved, but he had no time to react. He could hear the pounding of his heart. His eyes were wide, locked onto the masked men and all the guns pointed in his direction. Instinctively, he wanted to run, but where could he run to? Pinpoint laser beams all over his body and shouts of the police froze him in place.

After roughing Fuzz up a bit, the police threw him some pants and a t-shirt and ordered him to get dressed. Cuffed and shaking with fear, Fuzz was led out by the police to the waiting police van.

Fifteen minutes later, Fuzz was pulling up to the Police Administration Building, where they hustled him upstairs to Homicide Division and the interrogation room. Handcuffed to a metal chair that was bolted to the floor, Fuzz looked around the dimly-lit room. The only other furniture besides the chair was a metal table and another chair on the opposite side of the table. There were no windows, just dull, gray-painted walls. The room in itself was intimidating, but Fuzz was unafraid. *These motherfucker's don't know shit. Ain't nobody know nothing except me, Roach, and Busta. Roach ain't say nothing, and I know Busta ain't say shit. Or could he have?* Fuzz never got a chance to finish his thought. He heard the lock to the door click right before two detectives walked in.

"Christopher McMicheal, we got your ass cold, boy. Murder!" said the shorter of the two detectives.

"Murder? You got the wrong dude. I ain't kill nobody."

"Oh yeah? Well, in Pennsylvania we got what you call the felony homicide rule. What that is, is anytime a homicide happens in the commission of a felony, that's 2nd degree murder. The thing about 2nd degree that you probably don't know is, it's an automatic life sentence. Now I know when you hear the words life sentence, you're probably thinking about twenty or twenty-five years. And that's probably got you thinking about telling. But I'm about to give you even more incentive to cooperate. You see, in good ole PA, a life sentence means you never get out. Now ain't that just grand? Now just in case you a little slow, let me break that down for you. It means that the only way you get out of jail is if you die. Now just in case you still got a little fight in you, take a look at this." The short detective slid some papers across the desk towards Fuzz.

Fuzz picked the papers up and began to read. It was a statement from Bernadette. Sweat began to trickle down Fuzz's face. Realization dawned on him, they had him. *Fuck, I ain't know that bitch overheard me.*

"You got something you want to tell us?" said the other detective whose face was covered by so many pock marks it resembled a diaper rash. Diaper-Rash-Face could see the confidence drain from Fuzz's face. "You know you can get the death penalty for this, don't you? If I were you, I wouldn't take this case, especially for a motherfucker who, if they was in your shoes, would've been gave you up."

Fuzz could barely hear the detective. His mind was in overdrive, trying to come up with an idea to come up out of the dire straits he had found himself in. It didn't take long. The idea came to him like a flashbulb going off in a dark room. "Okay, if I tell y'all what y'all need to know, what's in it for me?"

"That's up to the D.A."

"Well, go get the D.A. then."

The detective left Fuzz in the room to go and let the D.A. know that Fuzz was ready to deal. Alone again, Fuzz began to formulate his plan. *I'ma give the case to Rafique. He was so high that night, he wouldn't know if he was there or not. This gonna be a perfect way to get that nigga out the way. If I say it was Roach, that crazy motherfucker might kill somebody in my family. Plus, him and Rafique look alike, especially if you don't really know them. That bitch Bernadette wouldn't know the difference. She was probably skitzing that night anyway.*

A few hours later, the D.A. arrived at the interrogation room. "Okay now, Mr. McMicheal, if your story pans out, you can plead out to a 3rd degree. You're gonna get some time, but I can get you like five years. Now before you say anything, the officer will advise you of your rights."

"Look, I'ma cooperate, but I'ma need something in writing."

The D.A. looked in his leather briefcase and pulled out some papers. He handed them to Fuzz. "This is the standard deal we give out for cooperating witnesses."

Fuzz looked over the papers. "Okay, now I'm ready to hear my rights."

Detective Diaper-Rash-Face spoke up: "You have the right to remain silent. Anything you say, can and will be used against you in a court of law. You have the right to an attorney. If you cannot afford one, one will be appointed to you. Do you understand these rights?"

"Yeah." Fuzz smiled and then began to weave his web of lies and half-truths. "I was shooting dice earlier that day with Righteous. He took all my money and was talking shit. I got mad and decided to get him robbed. After we were done gambling, I went to go see Busta, the dude who house Righteous be hustling out of. I let Busta know what I planned to do. Busta said he ain't care. After that, I walked up to 52nd Street and bumped into four dudes, Tashi, Buff, Ab, and Rafique. I asked Tashi, Buff, and Ab did they want to go get some money, but they said no. But then this dude Rafique said he wanted to go. I really didn't want to take him because he a little crazy, but then I just said fuck it. I had to get somebody to do it. So, me and Rafique left and we walked up to 54th Street. I then pointed the house out to him and told him where Righteous kept his money at. And then I told him I was gonna be parked on Spruce Street and that's where I would wait for him at. All he was supposed to do was rob him. I ain't have nothing to do with that shit once he turned it into something else. Anyway, about five minutes later, I heard a gunshot. Right after that, Rafique comes running down the street, talking about, 'I banged him.' I was like, 'what the fuck you do that for? All you had to do was smack him with the gun.' Rafique didn't say nothing so we got in the car, went to my house, and split the money and drugs up."

The D.A. was silent for a moment as he stared Fuzz in the eyes. He nodded his head, "Okay, look, until you testify in court you won't receive your sentence. Now like I told you, if you do well and we get a first- or second-degree conviction, on my word, you'll get five years."

Fuzz nodded his head, accepting the terms of the deal. After signing the necessary papers, Fuzz was pleased because he knew that he would do well and that five years was a done deal. He was able to relax. "Ay, Mr. D.A., you got a cigarette?"

The D.A. handed Fuzz a cigarette. "You can call me Mr. Brown. Mr. McMicheal, do you think you can pick this guy out of a photo spread?"

"Absolutely," Fuzz replied, blowing smoke rings into the air. The detective came in the room five minutes later with a book of mug shots. "Take your time and look through this," the detective said as he handed Fuzz the book. Fuzz opened the book and turned two pages before he looked up smiling. "There he go right there."

"Are you sure?" Mr. Brown said.

"Absolutely," Fuzz responded back while tapping his index finger repeatedly on Rafique's mug shot. And just like that, Rafique was a wanted murderer. Fuzz was then escorted downstairs to the bubble where he immediately headed for the phone. He picked up and dialed home. He needed to talk to his little brother. After getting his younger brother on the phone, Fuzz understood that once his brother hung up the phone, he would spread the lies throughout the neighborhood. Once that was done, Fuzz's lies would have a little validity. After all, the buzz was coming from the streets. It would only be a matter of time before one of the many police informants took the story back to the police, bringing the lie full circle and effectively cementing Rafique's future.

CHAPTER SIXTEEN

"Yo, Fuzz, you coming out? We getting ready to play spades and I need a partner," one of Fuzz's jailhouse friends hollered out, bringing Fuzz back up to the present and out of his memories.

"Naw, I ain't playing no cards. I got to get on the phone." Fuzz had been down for four months. The time had been frustrating for him because he had no trial date. He'd just been waiting for Rafique to be arrested so that he could get his time for testifying against him. Fuzz walked to the phone room with his head down, deep in thought. *I wish this nigga would get locked up. What if this nigga don't never get caught. These motherfuckers can take my deal back and take me to trial for this shit.* "That's time on that phone, my man," Fuzz said when he entered the phone room. The young man hung up the phone after a few minutes and walked out. Fuzz picked up the phone and dialed a number. He was calling a pay phone on the Strip. The phone rang in his ear while his mind fretted over Rafique getting locked up.

"Yo," a man's voice came over the line.
"Who this?" Fuzz asked.

"It's Peanut. Who this?"
"It's me, Fuzz."
"Damn, what's up, Fuzz?"
"It ain't nothing. I'm just trying to get the fuck out of here."
"Yo, Fuzz, your girl Lisa just walked past with that nigga Rafique. They was walking towards Market Street."
Fuzz clicked on the other line. He used the three-way feature on the phone to call the police. He was extremely careful not to click Peanut back on the line. No one could ever know that he was cooperating with the police.
"Police emergency. How can I help you?"
"Yeah, uh, I just saw this guy, he wanted for a murder. His name is Rafique Johnson. He on 52nd Street, walking towards Market."
"Sir, can you please..."
Fuzz didn't give the dispatch a chance to finish. He had clicked her off the line.
"Fuzz, what you just used the three-way to call somebody?"
"Yeah, I just called Lisa. To see if she was home with dude."
"Yo, Fuzz, I got to go. The police just got real thick out here and I'm dirty. If you can, try to call back a little later on."
"Alright, Nut, I'll holla at you later."
Fuzz hung up the phone feeling a lot better. *I hope they catch this nigga today.* Fuzz dialed another number. This time he called home. His little brother picked up. "Hello."
"Who this, Little Fuzz?"
"Yeah. Who this?"
"What the fuck you mean, 'Who this?' It's your big brother, chump. What's up?"

"Nothing. What's up with you?"
"I'm just trying to get the fuck out of here."
"Yeah?"
"Yeah. Listen, you know that nigga Rafique, right?"
"Yeah."
"Have you seen him around?"
"Naw, I ain't seen him."
"Alright, look, if you see him, you got to call the law on that nigga. You know they got me locked up for his body. When they get him, they gonna let me go."
"Straight up?"
"Yeah."
"Alright, if I see him I'ma call the law."
"Where Grandma at?"
"I don't know. She ain't here, though."
"Well, tell her I called. I'm out."
"Alright, Fuzz."

Fuzz hung up the phone, left out of the phone room, and joined the spades game.

✲ ✲ ✲

The bright lights of the Stop-N-Go deli beckoned all to stop and enter. Little Fuzz loitered outside the front door, waiting for someone to show up to make a beer run for him.

The Strip, as usual, was bustling with activity as crack fiends and hustlers did their thing to sell and consume misery in a small, plastic vial. Little Fuzz was in awe of the fast nightlife, and he wanted nothing more than to be just like what he perceived to be successful. He watched as the young hustlers pulled up in the latest cars, music blasting, jewels shining, immaculately dressed, and the finest women by their sides. This was his aspiration as he took the last swallow of the 40oz bottle of Old English he was drinking.

Mike, the Korean owner of the deli, banged on the front plate-glass window of his establishment, and in heavily accented English, he told Little Fuzz to beat it. Mike had a lucrative business and he couldn't afford to have his liquor license revoked as a result of this kid getting beer out of his establishment.

"Fucking chink. Non-talking motherfucker," Little Fuzz mumbled to himself as he slowly walked away to the corner and away from the front door.

It was eleven o'clock in the evening and Little Fuzz had just finished up his first forty. *I be glad when I'm twenty-one so I can get my own shit. There go Pine. I'ma get Pine to make a run for me.* "Yo, Pine, I need you to get this forty for me."

"You got a dollar?" Pine asked.

"Damn, man, yeah I got one."

The crack epidemic took a heavy toll on Pine. All he cared about was where the next dollar was coming from so that he could purchase bliss in a plastic vial. He didn't care about food, his hygiene, shelter, or even one of the most powerful urges a man in his prime years has, his sex drive. Crack overpowered all of these things. So he made a dollar anyway he could, even if it meant robbing, stealing, begging or simply making a beer run. Pine thought about taking the money from Little Fuzz, but then he thought better of it. He figured he would make out better doing the young boy a favor.

Pine exited the store and passed off the forty, collected his dollar, and left. Little Fuzz began walking towards Spruce Street, forty in hand, when he spotted Rafique coming off Delancey Street. *That's that nigga Rafique.*

Little Fuzz picked up his pace. He had to get home. He wanted his brother out of jail, so he had to call the police.

"911 emergency. May I help you?"

"Yeah, I just saw this guy, he wanted for a murder. His name is Rafique. I saw him on 52nd Street between Delancey and Larchwood."

"Okay, sir, where are you located?"

"My address is 5400 Delancey Street."

"Okay, a car will be there shortly."

Little Fuzz hung up the phone and went outside to wait on the police. The police arrived in five minutes. One of the officers got out of the car. "You the young man who called in about a fugitive?"

"Yeah, that was me."

"Okay, get in the car, we might need you to identify him."

Little Fuzz got into the car and the police pulled off, heading towards 52nd Street. A couple of short minutes later they were on 52nd Street. Little Fuzz saw that there were already about seven police cars already on the scene. Was that Rafique walking away? Little Fuzz began to panic. They couldn't let him get away. How would his brother get out then? "Excuse me, officer, but y'all letting him get away. There he go right there with that light-blue, silk jacket on."

Both officers jumped out the car and began to jog after Rafique. They caught up to him. Little Fuzz was relieved; he was able to do as his brother had asked. One of the officers grabbed Rafique from behind and spun him around towards the car. Little Fuzz nodded his head, indicating to the police that they had the right man. The police then put the handcuffs on Rafique. Little Fuzz couldn't hear, but he saw the officer who was holding

Rafique say something to the other officers. One of the officers opened up the police van, releasing another man. *Stupid motherfuckers had the wrong guy.* Little Fuzz smiled once they put Rafique into the police van. His brother would be coming home now.

Five minutes later, the police drove Little Fuzz home.

"You did a great service to your community, young man." The cop then handed Little Fuzz a card with a phone number, along with some other numbers. "Call this number and give the person this code so you can collect a reward. Good job."

Little Fuzz didn't care too much about doing a service to the community. He did want that reward money, though. But even more than that, he wanted them to let his brother go. Little Fuzz couldn't wait for his brother to call home so he could give him the good news.

CHAPTER SEVENTEEN

A week into his stay at Holmesburg, Rafique had a preliminary hearing. This hearing is for the District Attorney to present their evidence before a judge to see if it's strong enough for the case to go to trial.

Rafique walked into the courtroom and saw that there were two sections of seats separated by an aisle that ran down the middle of the room. There were at least ten rows on each side. Where the rows ended, there was a wooden partition waist high that separated the seating area from the defense and the prosecution tables, which were set up on opposite sides of the room. The whole set up was adversarial as if one side of the courtroom was against the other.

About ten feet separated the lawyer's tables from the judge's bench. The bench sat higher than anything else in the courtroom, creating an intimidating atmosphere. Below the judge's bench sat the stenographer, who, in shorthand, recorded everything that was being said during the hearing. On the left side of the judge was the witness box. Portraits of old white men hung on one of the walls of the courtroom, their faces frozen in time, their names all but forgotten, but their judgments buried in penitentiary graveyards across the state. Rafique took all this in as he approached the defense table. Already seated at the table was Rafique's court appointed attorney. "How are you? I'm Thomas Moore, the court has appointed me to represent you."

"What's up, man," Rafique responded as the sheriff uncuffed him. Rafique took a seat next Mr. Moore and stared straight ahead, waiting for the hearing to begin. A swarm of butterflies stirred in the pit of Rafique's gut. He was nervous. Who wouldn't be under these circumstances?

The hearing began when the prosecutors called their one and only witness, Bernadette Daniels.

"Do you swear to tell the truth and nothing but the truth so help you God?" Bernadette had her hand on a Bible as the bailiff swore her in.

"Ms. Daniels, can you recall the events of May 4, 1991?" This question was how the district attorney started the state's case.

Bernadette sat in the witness box and stared daggers at Rafique. She was a heavyset woman with very dark skin and a scar running through the right side of her cheek. She wore county prison blues that gave her a look of a woman who had led a hard life.

Rafique stared right back at her and he was puzzled. *Who the fuck is this? I ain't never seen this bitch before in my life.*

Bernadette cleared her throat and leaned forward. "Earlier during the day I was in Busta's house when Fuzz came up to the room. He asked to speak to Busta in private, so I left. I stayed right outside the door, though. The door was cracked, so I heard Fuzz say he was going to get Righteous robbed."

The D.A. cut in, "For the record, Righteous is the deceased. Please continue, Ms. Daniels."

"Well, later on that night, me, Righteous, Glenn, and Steve was sitting in the living room when somebody knocked on the door. Righteous got up to answer it. A couple minutes later, Righteous backed up into the vestibule. This guy had a gun on him. He was saying something."

"Who was saying something?" The D.A. asked.

"The guy with the gun," Bernadette responded, "I couldn't hear what he was saying, but when I saw that gun I ducked behind a chair. The next thing was, I heard a gunshot. When I looked up next, Righteous was on the floor and the guy was gone."

"Do you see the man who had the gun in the courtroom today?" The D.A. asked her.

"Yeah, I see him, he right there." Bernadette pointed at Rafique.

"For the record, the witness indicates the defendant."

Rafique's mind was in a blur, he was confused. *Who is this bitch?* Mr. Moore cross-examined Bernadette, but she stood fast and wouldn't budge from her story. After Mr. Moore exhausted all the questions he could think of, the defense rested. Finally, Bernadette could get off the stand.

The judge wasted no time in holding the case over for trail. Mr. Moore saw a look of extreme worry on Rafique's face. He leaned over and whispered in his client's ear, "This was to be expected. Don't worry about it. At trial we'll get to present your side of the story. I'll need to talk to you, so the sheriffs will bring you upstairs in a little while so we can meet. You okay?"

"Yeah, I'm cool." Rafique lowered his head as the sheriff put the cuffs on him and escorted him back to the holding cells.

An hour later, the sheriff picked him up again and took him to meet with Mr. Moore. Rafique was taken to a meeting room that was divided in half. One side for attorneys, the other for their clients. Mr. Moore was already seated on the opposite side of the room when Rafique entered. Rafique took a seat and faced him. Speaking through a wire-mesh screen, Mr. Moore got right to the point. "Look, I don't have a lot of time, I got to get back in court. I got your discovery here. When you get back to the jail, make sure you go over this. When you do, get back with me. You can call anytime between nine and five. The best time would be around four. So make sure you call after you go over these papers. The sheriff will give them to you after you leave out of here. You got any questions?"

Rafique shook his head.

"Well, alright, I'll hear from you soon." With that said, Mr. Moore got up and left.

Later on that day, Rafique was back at the Burg, sitting in his cell and going over his discovery. Not knowing what it was, Rafique learned that it was all the evidence the district attorney would be using to convict him. It had all of the statements that were made concerning the homicide: witness statements, medical reports, interviews, warrants, and ballistics. There were about eight different witness statements, two of which identified him as the killer - Fuzz's statement and the statement by Bernadette.

After reading all the statements, Rafique began to get a mental picture of what had happened that night, but none of it stirred his memory.

"920053," the guard called down the block.

Rafique got up and walked to the front of the block where the guard station was located. "Yo, you just called my number?"

"You 920053?"

"Yeah."

"You got a visit."

Rafique took the visiting pass from the guard's outstretched hand. Just like school, a pass was the only way you could move around the jail. Rafique left the block and proceeded to the visiting room.

When he arrived he had to change from his blue uniform to an orange jumpsuit. After changing, he entered the visiting room. A low murmur of voices greeted his ears as he walked into the room. The next thing he noticed was how brightly colored the room was painted: orange, yellow, light blue, and green. It was as if the colors could somehow change the atmosphere of an otherwise gloomy place. The colors didn't work. No matter how bright the colors were, they did nothing to change the depressiveness of the circumstances. Rafique looked to his left and then to his right. He scanned the room, looking for his visitor. He didn't see anyone, so he took a chair and waited for them to enter. The room was filled with prisoners and their loved ones, mostly women and children. There were seats lined up against the walls and in the middle of the room. The way it was set up it resembled the waiting room of a bus station. Rafique continued to observe his surroundings. His mother, followed by his two younger sisters Kim and Kalima, his brother Masai, and finally, his daughter Shante, entered the room. He hadn't seen any of them since he went on the run. Seeing them made Rafique realize how much he missed them.

"Hey, Mom." Rafique gave his mother a big hug. He then turned and embraced his siblings before turning to his little girl. He hugged her tight and kissed her on the forehead. "Hey, baby girl. I missed you."

Shante was the spitting image of her father. She had the complexion of a Hershey Kiss, and she had slanted eyes, and long, black, wavy hair. Shante shied away from her father as if he were a stranger. She wouldn't respond when he tried to talk to her. She even wiped his kiss away. Rafique was hurt, but he understood what the problem was. After all, he experienced with his father exactly what she was feeling now. He understood that he had spent too much time away from her, and as a result she didn't feel comfortable around him. Rafique wanted to press her, but he didn't. He knew that the only way for him to conquer what she was feeling was to give her time and to see her as much as possible. He turned to his mother. "Mom, can you please try to bring her up here as much as possible? You see how she is with me? Only time and my presence can fix this."

Tonya nodded her head. She understood as well.

"So, Mom, what's up? Is everything okay?"

"Everything's fine, Rafique. I'm just worried about you."

"I'm doing okay. There's no need to worry about me."

"No need to worry? What about this case? I knew taking those pills and drinking that syrup would get you in a world of trouble. I just wish you had listened to me. Do you think that you were the first person this has happened to? Baby, I tried to protect you from this. I've been on this planet twice as long as you and I've seen this kind of shit before. Look at all your uncles in and out of jail. You had a family of examples. Why didn't you listen?"

Rafique sat in silence. He didn't know the answer. The questions his mother just asked he had been asking himself for weeks now. Why didn't he listen? Why didn't he learn from his uncle's mistakes? Rafique's eyes were glued to the floor. He just didn't know what to say. Slowly, he lifted his head. "Mom, I don't know. I've been asking myself the same questions. I just don't know, maybe something's wrong with me. Maybe in time I'll figure it out. But right now I need to figure out how to beat this case. I had a preliminary hearing today. Some girl got on the stand, and to make a long story short, she said I killed the dude. So they are holding my case over for trial. I met my lawyer today, his name is Thomas Moore. Don't you have a friend that's a lawyer?"

Tonya nodded her head.

"Well, can you holla at him and see if he know this dude? I still got some money out DC. Call Pluck, he'll give up whatever I need if I need to get a lawyer. The lawyer did give me my discovery. That's the thing with all the statements in it. I was just reading it when they called me to come down here."

"So who's making statements against you?"

"Well, like I said, some girl named Bernadette and this dude named Fuzz. The girl is the eyewitness and Fuzz is locked up on the case, too. He's saying that he set the robbery up and I went in the house and instead of just robbing the dude, I killed him. He took a deal to testify against me. The thing is, I know Fuzz, but I don't know him. I mean, I never dealt with this dude. I barely even speak to him. Damn, I wish I could remember what happened."

Time flew by as Rafique and his mother discussed the case. Before you knew it, the guard had walked over. "Times up, Mr. Johnson."

"Damn, that was a quick hour," Rafique said as he stood up and began hugging his family members. "Look, y'all, I'm sorry I ain't get a chance to talk to y'all too much, but me and Mommy had some important things to talk about. It's only an hour visit, but the next time is all about y'all." Rafique looked at his little girl. He picked her up. "I love you, baby girl." He gave her a kiss on the cheek.

Shante turned her head away, frowned her face, and wiped his kiss off again. Pain shot through his body like a adrenaline rush, and he could do nothing right now to affect this situation. "Mom, you see this, right? Please help me get my daughter back."

"I will, baby, don't worry about it."

After some more hugs and kisses, Rafique's family left the visiting room. Rafique left out feeling real good about seeing his family, only to have that feeling erased by the humiliating ass-crack search.

Once back on the block, Rafique went straight to his cell. Angel was asleep so he walked lightly to his bunk. He looked down, and on his bed was a letter addressed from his father.

✯ ✯ ✯

IN THE NAME OF ALLAH THE BENEFICENT
THE MERCIFUL
Assallamu Alaikum Wa Rahmatullahi Wa Barakatuh

Oh my son, I never wanted to have to write to you under these circumstances, but such is the life of this world we live in. Sometimes things don't always go as we planned them. I'm happy only because you're still alive, that means that Allah has given you another chance at this life. You know I always considered you one of the geniuses of the family; this is why you frustrated me so much, because I knew you could do anything. This is still true today so I beg you now take advantage of this time, get to know yourself, not just as a black man in America but also as one of Allah's creations endowed with a creative mind, a soul, and a strong and enduring will. Take this time to love yourself, dwell on the benefits of a good sound mind and a strong body, a mother who loves you, and a father who loves you as well. Love yourself, we have always loved you and believed in you.

I want you to understand that neither your mother nor I were mature enough when you were born to understand the difficulties that our separation would cause you, but you must also understand that even if we had stayed together the probability is that your life would still contain the same level of difficulties. Difficulties, problems, hurts, and disappointments are the learning tools of this life. If a child sticks his hand in the fire and is burned, thereafter he knows the fire is hot. I'm preparing to send you the books you need. Do you have your Quran? I love you Rafique. I am in your corner, write to me. You mother will be coming up to see you for that one hour per week. I'll come when she lets me. Write to me Rafique I know that you are going through a lot right now, but have faith, Allah will see you through. Look I've got to end this letter for now but I'll write again soon.

May Allah guide you; try to make your prayers. The books will follow soon.

Love your father,
Jamil

CHAPTER EIGHTEEN

The raucous sounds of hundreds of voices were a discordant jumble of noise that invaded Rafique's peace and filled the confines of the cell block. He got up feeling irritated and turned the volume up on his transistor radio. The music wasn't loud enough to drown out the chatter completely, but it was enough to help him blank it out. Rafique walked back to his bunk, lay down, and closed his eyes. Automatically, his mind began to take stock of his present situation. He was being held in the most notorious county prison in Pennsylvania for a crime he had no memory of. Over the last six months, Rafique had been in a continued state of disbelief. Just a short two years ago he would have never imagined that his life would take this kind of turn. But, yet, here he was without a clue as to how to get things right.

Rafique's stress level was high. Not only was he worried about his case, but he had to stay on point. In the Burg, outbursts of violence were a guarantee. Imagine living in an enclosed space with hundreds of young men, their bloodstreams flooded with the aggression-fueled chemical testosterone, all of them on trial for some very serious crimes. On top of all these factors, the most deadly ingredient of them all was a part of this mix: perception. For Rafique and the rest of the young men who resided at Holmsburg county prison, perception shaped reality. How they saw the world dictated their behavior. Most of the young men had a perception of prison before they entered one. These warped views based off tall tales and sensationalized TV shows became real as the young men behaved in ways that their realities deemed appropriate - when in Rome, act like the Romans.

Just like the ancient city of Rome, the Burg had its own coliseum where the gladiator sport took place: the phone room. The different geographical locations of the city were divided into cliques: West and Southwest Philly, North Philly, South Philly, and Germantown. This added more stress to an already tense atmosphere, and the direct-line phones brought this situation to its breaking point. Most of the fights and stabbings took place because of the phones. You couldn't step into the phone room without a weapon; to enter you had to be prepared. Each cell block had a phone room with four direct lines and two collect-call phones. Each section of the city had at least one phone for their section. For the general population of the block, if they were lucky enough to be on a block that allowed usage of the direct lines, it usually ran in the mornings for two hours with ten minute time slots. So if you were one of those guys who didn't belong to a group, you had to rise with birds to use the direct-line phones, or you just didn't use one.

Gang wars flared up all the time because one section of the city felt like they weren't getting their fair share of phone time, so it was always tense. There was never a relaxing moment at the Burg, and this was Rafique's world. He adapted quickly, but that adaptation came at a price. Rafique became so engrossed with surviving his circumstance that he wasn't preparing himself for his upcoming trial. Rafique could never fully see that his life was on the line. He would pay dearly for this shortsightedness.

Meanwhile, his mother had talked to her lawyer friend and was told that Thomas Moore was a good attorney. This information was another nail in Rafique's coffin because it made it easier for him not to prepare. Rafique put his life in Thomas Moore's hands. Rafique had a lot to learn and the lesson would start soon.

"Medication!" A few days later, the C/O's call down the block for medication awakened Rafique out of a restless sleep. He jumped out the bed and went to the phone room to call his attorney.

"Yo, my man, that's time on that phone." Rafique tensed up and gripped the taped-up handle of his makeshift knife, just in case the young man didn't comply. The young man nodded his head and Rafique relaxed. The young man hung up the phone and handed the phone to Rafique.

"Mr. Moore and associates, how can I help you?" Thomas Moore's secretary answered after several rings.

"Hello, is uh, Thomas Moore in?"

"No he's not. May I ask who's calling?"

"This, uh, Rafique Johnson."

"Mr. Johnson, he left word to tell you that you start trial on Monday."

"What? I haven't even talked to him yet."

"Well, he's coming to see you tonight."

"Hold up, today is Friday. Why would he wait three days before I start trial to come see me?"

"That's something you'll have to discuss with him, goodbye."

"Hold up, wai..." The phone went dead as Rafique tried to question the secretary further. Rafique stared at the phone in disbelief. He thought about calling back, but then changed his mind. *I'll just wait and see this motherfucker tonight.*

Later on that evening, Rafique received a visit from his attorney. Rafique walked into the visiting area reserved for attorney visits and spotted Mr. Moore immediately. Mr. Moore stood about six-feet-three, he was strikingly thin, he looked to have weighed about one-hundred and fifty pounds soaking wet. Rafique shook his head. *This motherfucker probably getting high.* Rafique began to doubt what his mother's attorney friend had told his mother about Mr. Moore being a good attorney. Rafique approached him and shook his hand. After they were seated, Mr. Moore began the conversation by asking, "What happened?"

"I don't know what happened. I don't even know if I was even there. I was high off some Valiums. I took about ten of them jawns that night."

Mr. Moore had a look of total disbelief on his face. He checked his watch.

"Yo, man, you looking at me like you don't believe me or something. If you don't believe me, all you gotta do is go down 52nd Street. It be plenty of dudes on that corner. 9 out of 10 of them was out there that night. I know if you go down there you'll find somebody that can help me."

"Do you have any names?"

"Yeah."

"I think we're going to have to use diminished capacity defense."

"What's that?"

"It's when you're not in your right state of mind from taking drugs or a mental disorder, and as a result of that, you do something you wouldn't normally do."

"Naw, fuck no, we ain't doing that. If we do that, then I'll be saying that I did it. Excuse my language, but fuck that!"

"Okay, whatever you want," Mr. Moore said, looking at his watch again. "It's getting late and I have some Christmas shopping I need to do. I'll definitely go down 52nd Street and talk to some people." Mr. Moore stood up. "So I'll see you on Monday." Mr. Moore extended his hand and shook Rafique's, before he turned and left the visiting room.

✯ ✯ ✯

"Mr. Rafique Johnson, would you please stand. We the jury find you guilty of murder in the first degree, and we sentence you to death."

The pounding of Rafique's heart was all that he could hear as he sat up in the middle of the night, body soaked in sweat. *Shit, it was only a dream.* Rafique got out of bed, walked to the sink, and splashed cold water on his face. He then lay back down and tried to force himself to sleep. It was to no avail, because on this night, sleep was as elusive as Michael Vick avoiding an all-out blitzing pass rush. So Rafique was awake when the C/O came pass shining a flashlight in his eyes. "920053, you got court."

"I'm up, man. Get that light out of my face."

"You can go ahead and take a shower. When you get dressed, go to the front of the block, an officer will be there to pick you up."

After the guard left, things moved quickly. Four hours flew by like four minutes. Before Rafique knew it, he was on the top floor of City Hall, sitting in a holding cell, waiting his turn to be called to court.

The dimly-lit holding cell was full to capacity as Rafique sat on the bench with his eyes closed trying to ease his nerves.

"Yo, Fuzz, what's up man?"

Rafique's head jerked up and his eyes flew open. *Fuzz? Is that nigga in here?* Rafique's eyes slowly inspected the cell. Fuzz was not there. Rafique stood up and looked to the cell next to the one he was in. There he was, Fuzz, talking as if he didn't have a care in the world.

This motherfucker. "Yo, Fuzz!"

Fuzz had a smile on his face, but when he looked up at hearing his name being called and saw Rafique, that smile instantly evaporated. Fuzz was tentative when he answered. "What's up, Fique? I don't know why they got me down here." Fuzz didn't know that Rafique had his statement and a copy of the deal he made with the D.A.

"You don't know why you down here? Is you serious? Motherfucker, I'm on trial! That's why you the fuck down here! Nigga, you testifying against me! Stop acting like you don't know what the fuck is going on!"

"Rafique, man, you put me in a fucked up position. You wasn't supposed to shoot that nigga. They was talking about giving me the death penalty for that shit. What was I supposed to do?"

"I got to tell you what to do? Bite that shit, nigga! That's what you supposed to do."

The holding cells were deathly quiet as Rafique and Fuzz went back and forth.

"Christopher McMichael!" The sheriffs realized their mistake of putting Fuzz with the rest of the prisoners going to court.

Fuzz heard his name and immediately got up. He walked to the front of the holding cell, never once looking back.

Rafique shook with anger, but there was nothing he could do. Not five minutes had passed by before they were calling him. Rafique got up and walked to the front of the holding cell where he was handcuffed and led to the courtroom.

Rafique was oblivious to the sights and sounds around him as he was being escorted through the corridors of City Hall. His mind was being blitzed by a thousand images as he sorted through every moment that led up to this point. As the courtroom got closer, he tried to prepare himself for what lay ahead, but it was impossible. His heart hammered against his rib cage, his hands began to sweat, and his mouth was bone-dry. Rafique was more than nervous as a paralyzing fear shot through his body. At that precise moment, Rafique began to see what was at stake.

Rafique entered the courtroom and saw that it was jam-packed. On one side of the courtroom were his family and friends. His mother and father were in the front row, along with his brothers and sisters. He spotted Shawn and the rest of his close friends, along with all of his aunts and uncles. Someone was missing though. Rafique squinted his eyes, looking for his daughter, but she was nowhere in sight. Maybe it was better that she wasn't there, he thought. As soon as the sheriff uncuffed him, Rafique turned and waved to all of his supporters. He didn't smile. This wasn't a happy time as he kept his face impassive, concealing all of the emotions that were boiling inside of him. Rafique turned back around and took his seat.

"All rise. The Honorable Judge O'Keefe is entering the courtroom," the bailiff called out.

Everyone in the courtroom stood up as an old white man entered. The judge, his black robe flowing in his wake, took his seat high up on the bench, and without looking up he asked, "Counsel, is this a waiver trial?"

"Yes, your Honor," responded Mr. Moore. "May I have a word with my client?"

"Yes you may."

Mr. Moore turned to Rafique. "Alright look, I think it would be in your best interest to go straight up with this judge. A jury is too emotional. Besides, this is a very fair judge."

Rafique had confidence in Mr. Moore, so he agreed to waive his right to be tried by a jury of his peers, which turned out to be a fatal mistake. After the judge read the colloquy, an instruction that explains what it is when you give up your right to be judged by a jury, the trial began.

The trial didn't last very long. It began on the twenty-third of December and was over on the twenty-fourth, just in time for the Christmas holiday.

Bernadette testified about what she saw and overheard. Fuzz got on the stand and testified about his part in the robbery, but he blamed Rafique for the murder. Mr. Moore turned out to be terribly unprepared. He never went to 52nd Street to interview anyone, so he didn't have any witnesses. All he did was cross-examine the witnesses that the prosecution presented.

After the closing arguments, the judge didn't even retire to his chambers to give his judgment any more consideration. He simply said, "Mr. Johnson, would you please stand?" The judge paused, giving Rafique a moment to stand. "I find you guilty of murder in the 2nd degree, which carries a mandatory-minimum sentence of life without the possibility of parole."

Rafique was stunned as a rush of emotion flooded his being: anger, for allowing himself to be put in a position where other people had complete control over his life. And sadness, because the most precious right a human being can possess, the right to be free, was taken away from him, possibly for the rest of his life.

The judge kept talking but his words were unintelligible on account of the heart-wrenching wail that erupted from Rafique's mother's vocal chords. When Rafique heard his mother scream, he felt a pain so intense, so sharp, so unforgiving that it was as if his soul had been ripped through the tears that were struggling to break free from the prison of his eyes. At that moment, Rafique turned to the sheriff, "Yo, man, please get me the fuck out of here."

The sheriff obliged him and hurriedly put the cuffs on Rafique's wrist before escorting him out the courtroom. Rafique entered the hallway, head bowed and struggling hard to keep the tears at bay. He heard someone crying, which cause him to look up. It was his sister Kim, her face awash in tears, and sobs racking her body. At that moment, Rafique felt a sadness he had never felt in his entire life. Not because he had been found guilty, but because of all the pain he caused the people that loved him. It was as at that point that he realized that life and how he lived it affected not only him, but other people as well. The tears that he had been holding back finally broke free. Rafique couldn't incarcerate them any longer. The tears, free of their imprisonment, ran free, covering his face with the signs of their escape.

Rafique entered the holding cell to silence. The other prisoners could tell by the tears streaming down his face that things didn't go well for him. No one said a word. They all sat quietly consumed by their own fears until the bus picked them up for the trip back to Holmesburg.

Back at the prison, word got out that Rafique had been found guilty and given a life sentence. A few of his friends stopped by to see if he was doing okay, but most of the guys just stayed away. Rafique only stayed at Holmesburg for six more days, and on December 30, 1992 he was back on the Blue Goose prison bus, headed for upstate.

CHAPTER NINETEEN

Rafique could see the prison wall from afar. It loomed large, beckoning as if it were built specifically for him. He was on his way to Graterford State Penitentiary. Built in the early 1900's, it was the fifth-largest prison in the country. It was located in Montgomery County, Pennsylvania, right outside of Philadelphia's city limits, forty-five minutes by car. In 1992 when Rafique first arrived, it had a population of close to five thousand men.

Rafique's heart pounded against his chest cavity as the bus pulled in front of the forty-foot wall. Seagulls circled high above, their cries were the only sound Rafique could hear above the chatter of nervous voices on the bus. The feeling of anxiousness made his stomach queasy as he stared at the huge wall. *Now this is jail.* Rafique began recalling all the stories he had heard about the murders, the stabbings, and the rapes. Rafique took a deep breath as he began to prepare himself mentally to do whatever was necessary to survive. Once inside the prison, he was issued the basic necessities and then escorted to a room where a young female correctional officer sat behind a desk cluttered with paper. Before she spoke, Rafique took notice of her name tag, C/O M. Thompson.

"Rafique Johnson, I see you have a life sentence. Would you mind if I ask you a personal question?"

Rafique was caught off guard. He frowned before nodding his head.

"The person you're locked up for, was he black or white?"

Wrinkles deepened in Rafique's forehead. He was puzzled by the question, more so out of curiosity than anything else. He answered, "He was black."

"Well, you probably won't have to do all that time, you'll probably get it overturned on appeal. So you can get back out there and kill more black people. Now if he was white, that would be a whole different story. You would be in here for every second of that sentence. Okay, now, where do you want your body sent?"

"What? Why you asking me that?"

"I'm asking you this because, first of all, it's my job. Secondly, it ain't guaranteed that you gonna make it out of here alive. After all, you do have a life sentence."

Hearing the guard say those words shook Rafique to his core. Although Rafique knew what his situation was, to him it was as if he was watching the situation happen to someone else. At hearing the guard voice it, though, made it all come crashing home. This situation wasn't happening to someone else, it was happening to him. Rafique cleared his throat, "You can send it to my mother." It was strange hearing himself talk about his own body as if it weren't about him. Rafique dropped his head, his mind on automatic as he answered the guard's questions without giving them much thought. He was in another world as all of his anxieties bore down on him.

After that encounter, Rafique continued through the intake process, and before long, he was sent to the new side of the prison. The new-side was an extension to the prison recently built in the late 1980's to accommodate the war-on-drugs prison-population explosion. Rafique was housed on upper F block where all the new arrivals and parole violators were housed.

As soon as he got on the block, the block officer assigned him to a cell, and he immediately headed there. Rafique arrived at the cell door and looked inside. The cell was already occupied. He knocked before entering. "What's up? I'm your new celly."

The young man turned and Rafique immediately recognized him. "Damn, what's up, Mark?"

"What's up, Fique?"

Mark was a guy he knew from 52nd Street. The two friends shook hands before Rafique sat his box down.

"Ay, Mark, I got three uncles here. How do I get word to them that I'm here?"

"You got to send word over by the block workers. They live on the old-side, but they work over here. I'll show you who they are tomorrow. How much time they give you?"

"They gave me a life sentence, man."

"Life! Damn, man, and I was sitting up here bitching about this punk-ass violation I got."

"So what's up with this jawn?"

"Fique, man, this the place to be, especially if you doing a lot of time. You know they call this jawn 'The Party.' Shit, it's wide open down here. Don't get me wrong, it ain't sweet like that. A motherfucker will hurt you."

"Yo, do niggas be getting raped in here?"

"I'ma tell you like this. If a motherfucker getting fucked, it's because he want to get fucked. Don't believe all that shit you be hearing. Look, man all you got to do is mind your business and try not to get hooked up in all the jailhouse bullshit that be going on. Stay focused on what's important, and that's getting the fuck out of here. Look, man, you going to be alright, you ain't no nut, you know how to bid. You'll only be here for a minute, though, you got to go up Camp Hill to get classified. They'll send you to the jail you're going to be doing your time at. Hopefully, they'll send you back down here. You don't want to be in those other jails up in those mountains, trust me." The next day, Mark showed Rafique who the block workers were and he was able to get a message to his uncles. Later that day he received a pass to report to the Lieutenant's Office. Rafique arrived at the Lieutenant's Office and walked up on all three of his uncles, Joe-Joe, Duck, and Wease. He hadn't seen Joe-Joe or Duck since he was about ten years old. Wease was just a parole violator, so he was just on the streets with him. Still, he was glad to see all three of them. Rafique embraced and shook all of their hands. His Uncle Joe looked at him. "Yo, we got to make this quick, we only got fifteen minutes. Rafique, when you get to Camp Hill, tell them you want to come here."

"Do you need anything?" Duck asked.

"Yeah, I need some cigarettes."

"I'ma send you over some tonight," Wease chimed in.

"Look, man, make sure you go to the law library. Just because you got that life sentence don't mean that you stop fighting. As long as you got breath in your body, you fight to get your freedom back, you dig?" Duck said, putting his arm on Rafique's shoulder. They talked until fifteen minutes later when the lieutenant came out of an office and reminded them that their time was up.

"Look, man, we see you when you get back down here." Joe-Joe said, embracing him.

"Alright, y'all, I'll see y'all when I get back down here." Rafique embraced his uncles one by one before turning and heading back to the cell block.

That night of December 31, 1992, Rafique lay on the top bunk and listened as the other prisoners hollered out of their cells, counting down to midnight. Shouts of "Happy New Year" rang out as Rafique lay irritated on his bunk. *What the fuck is wrong with these niggas? How can you be happy locked in a fucking cell?*

Just like Mark said, two weeks later Rafique was transferred to Camp Hill. When they pulled up to Camp Hill on the Blue Goose, Rafique noticed that the prison didn't have a wall. Instead, it was surrounded by a large fence, topped with rows of razor wire. There were also towers manned by armed guards. Rafique would find out soon that Camp Hill was a rough spot for more reasons than one.

Fresh off the 1989 riots, the guards were still acting out their revenge. Filled with racist views and stereotypes that had been fostered for generations, these racist views were expressed at every given opportunity. Rafique was astonished by the hate. For Rafique, racism was something that was more like an idea instead of a reality. He was definitely aware of it. After all, he was a child of the seventies. But being aware and actually being dropped smack dead in the middle of it was something entirely different. Due to the fact that the county prison was within the city limits and Graterford was in close proximity to the city, Rafique was used to being around guards who disliked him because he broke a law. It was more of a self-righteous kind of hate. Rafique was used to black guards who came out of the same neighborhoods as he did. For the most part, they treated him with the respect that any human being has a right to. Even with the white guards, although there was an element of racism, it was different; it was a bit more subtle.

Camp Hill was the first stop on the Penitentiary Express. This was where Rafique got his first taste of life outside Graterford's walls. Pennsylvania is probably one of the most racist states in the country. There are more hate groups in Pennsylvania than any state in the union. The Aryan Nation had just moved their national headquarters to Pennsylvania, giving true meaning to the nickname "Keystone State." Most of the recruits from these hate groups came from the rural counties where most of these prisons are. These same recruits get hired as guards, a perfect recipe for abuse. These guards not only hate prisoners because they're prisoners, they also hate them because they're black. The few weeks that Rafique had at Camp Hill couldn't go by fast enough. During Rafique's stay at Camp Hill, he had to go through a classification process that required him to be tested physically as well as psychologically. The time he had for himself he spent studying the law and reading the Quran. Rafique began making his prayers five times a day, a daily Muslim obligation, but it was something that he had gotten away from, and now Rafique was beginning to make wholesale changes in his life. He understood now that the way he had been living previously had gotten him into the situation he was in, which wasn't good, so to change could only mean to improve.

Several weeks had passed at Camp Hill and Rafique was almost at the breaking point. He was tired of the disrespect, the racist jokes, and the daily humiliations. Sitting in his cell, he was trying to get some measure of peace by reading his Quran when he was interrupted by a guard calling out his new state ID number. He looked up and saw the guard standing at his cell with a pass in his hand. "BZ-9999, you got a pass."

Rafique got up and walked to the cell door to retrieve his pass. He then proceeded to the destination. When he got there, he entered a medium-sized, dull beige-painted room. There were two windows with cheap brown curtains that overlooked the main yard. The curtains were drawn, allowing the sunshine to pour in to light up the room. The only furniture in sight was an empty metal chair and a long wooden table. A small group of people, six white men and one white woman, sat behind the table.

"BZ-9999, would you please take a seat." The man who spoke was very pale and bald, and to Rafique, looked to be the oldest of the group. He paused as Rafique sat down in the chair that faced the table. "We've called you here today because you're going to be assigned to the jail you'll be doing your time at. Okay now, what jail would you like to go to?"

Rafique didn't answer right away. *Shit, I get to choose?* "Muncy." Muncy was a women's prison.

"Mr. Johnson, I see you have a sense of humor. You're going to Graterford. Sorry we couldn't be more accommodating," the woman said with a smile on her face.

Rafique was okay with that decision. He figured if he couldn't go to a women's prison, the next best thing was Graterford.

"Okay, Mr. Johnson, you can leave now," the woman continued.

Rafique left out the room and went back to his cell. As soon as he stepped in, he saw a letter addressed from his father lying on the floor.

✯ ✯ ✯

IN THE NAME OF ALLAH THE BENEFICENT
THE MERCIFUL
Assallamu Alaikum Wa Rahmatullahi Wa Barakatuh

Oh my son, I did something after your trial today as I traveled by train back to Washington. I cried; I cried because I felt helpless in the face of a threat to my family. I realized again that free men can't be slaves, and slaves can't be free men. I cried because I love my children and want them to cherish their freedom, to understand it, to protect it, and to maintain it. I cried because you didn't understand me and therefore fought me, placing yourself in the hands of those who envy you, who despise you, and because of their envy seek at every opportunity to steal from you your birthright, your freedom. This birthright, this gift, your freedom, is best maintained through knowledge. So as I read your letter that I received today I cried again, because now you seem to understand me and what I went through and what I was desperately trying to get you to understand. The feelings you now feel, I felt too, the loneliness, the rejection, the defeat, the fear, all these feelings are what, if faced honestly makes a person come to a sense of who he is. When you face yourself and look at all the parts that make you who you are and you accept what you see and learn how to love and appreciate all those parts of yourself no matter how they appear, then and only then are you free.

TERREL CARTER

Now I think we can talk, but you must write often. You are correct in your decision to study the law. I am aware of the fact that some kind of conspiracy took place at your trial between your lawyer, the prosecutor, and the judge. The case was weak at best and your lawyer didn't want to waste time with a jury trial. Time is money in the law business. There was no deliberation at all by the judge, as if your life wasn't worth his thinking about.

Work must be you priority, you're in the big boy club now. Life can be rough, work on your writing, be careful, extra careful with who you affiliate with. Those who profess to be your friends can be your worst enemies. Examine the self, free yourself from the prison of your mind, the prison you created through self-doubt, fear, and the feelings of rejection.

Stone walls do not a prison make nor iron bars a cage. Prison is in your mind.

Assallamu Alaikum
With love Jamil

CHAPTER TWENTY

December 1982

The glow from the burning cigarettes was like pinpricks of light in the dimly-lit bar. Secondhand smoke rose lazily to the ceiling, polluting the air. A low murmur of the thin crowd could be heard just above the pounding of the drum beat as the jukebox blared. Some of the patrons whispered quietly amongst each other about their week-long stresses. Some flirted with the opposite sex in search of one-night stands, while others danced to the new form of music that was sweeping inner cities across the country.

FEEL THE HEART BEAT, FEEL THE HEART BEAT,
WE'RE THE TREACHEROUS THREE,
WE GOT A NEW HEARTBEAT ...

Big Moose, nodding his head in rhythm with the music, sat alone in a corner booth of the Cozy Nook Bar, drinking a rum and coke. He glanced at this watch for the tenth time in less than five minutes. *Where the fuck is she?* He had been waiting for his girlfriend Shelly. She was over a half hour late. Big Moose was one of the leaders of the street gang called The Moon Gang, located in West Philadelphia at 60th and Market Street. Big Moose was one of the leaders, not because he was particularly smart, not because of his good looks, but because he was six-foot-four and two hundred and forty pounds of solid muscle. With power in both hands, he could knock you out with one punch, right or left. This was how he ascended to a leadership position by leaving a trail of broken jaws and knockout victims.

On this cold wintery Saturday night, Big Moose was the only one of his gang in the bar, which was cool because the Cozy Nook was in the heart of his gang's territory and no other gang would dare venture this deep into their domain. Moose checked his cheap Timex for the eleventh time. He frowned once more. *Mmmaaann, where the fuck is she at?* Moose took a sip of his drink as a cool breeze left an icy kiss on the nape of his neck. The front door to the bar had opened and closed. Moose, hoping that it was Shelly, turned and faced the door. Shelly was nowhere in sight. But what he did see made him forget all thoughts of Shelly. Standing in the doorway were Bolo and Tone, two young men from Cedar Avenue, a rival gang from the south side. Moose was outraged. *Who the fuck these niggas think they is coming up in here like this?* Big Moose stood up and walked towards his two rivals.

"What's up?" Bolo spoke at seeing Moose approach.

Big Moose didn't respond, he just kept walking towards the two. Bolo was the bigger of the two men at six-feet and two hundred pounds. He hated Moose and came up to the bar specifically to pick a fight. Bolo turned to Tone. "Step back, homie, I got this." As Moose got closer, Bolo prepared himself for battle. The bar patrons scattered for fear of getting in the way of this heavyweight brawl. The barmaid picked up the phone and called the cops.

Moose never broke his stride, and when he got in punching range he threw a wicked straight right hand, catching Bolo flush on the chin and knocking him out instantly. Bolo fell hard, hitting his head on the pointy edge of a pinball machine, causing his brain to hemorrhage. Moose wasn't done. Not knowing that Bolo was critically wounded, he began to stomp him. Tone stood by petrified, watching as his best friend was beat to death. Just as Moose got his last kick in, the police burst through the door. "Freeze! Get your fucking hands in the air!" Moose was in a blind rage and the shouts of the police fell on deaf ears. The police rushed him, but Moose was ready. One by one the police hit the floor. Never really needing an excuse to use deadly force, the police opened fire, hitting him five times. Moose woke up a few days later in the hospital, tubes running everywhere and handcuffed to the bed. A lone police officer sat across from him, reading a newspaper. He saw that Moose was awake. He put the newspaper down walked over to the bed. He bent over and leaned close to Moose's ear. "Well, well, well, the big-ass nigger has finally awakened." Moose was feeling the effects of the pain medication, so his response wasn't coherent.

"What you say now, darkie?" the police officer said, leaning close to Moose again. Moose didn't respond because sleep had claimed him once again.

✭ ✭ ✭

MARCH 1993

Eleven years had passed and Big Moose's release date was at hand. As he walked up the prison block, he said his goodbyes to his gang. Eleven years ago he had been sentenced to ten-to-twenty years for the death of Bolo. Time seemed to crawl by for him, but now that it was over it seemed like it was only yesterday. As he continued to walk up the block, his heart rate increased as his anxiety levels rose.

"Damn, Duck, I can't believe this shit is over," Moose said, turning to Duck as he walked him up the block.

"Yeah, I know. Just don't come back."

"Shit, nigga, you seen the scars. That's the only way they gonna bring me back in this motherfucker."

The two friends arrived at the front of the block, shook hands, and embraced before Moose turned and left. Duck watched Moose as he walked off the block to his freedom. *I wonder if he gonna be like the rest of these motherfuckers that leave here and forget about the rest of us still here. Moose, that's my man, we walked up and down this motherfucker for eleven years. He gonna look back, I know it.*

When Moose got outside the prison walls, he let out a yell, "Fuck Graterford!" He then bent down and kissed the ground. *I'm free. I can't believe this shit.* As Moose stood up, a black Limited Edition Cherokee slowly pulled up next to him and the driver's-side tinted window slowly rolled down. Moose looked into the car. "Do I know you?"

"Yeah, nigga, it's me, Cliff."

"Goddamn, young buck, I ain't seen you since you was a snotty-nose, little nigga asking me for quarters. Plus, you don't look nothing like them pictures you was sending up here."

During the past eleven years Moose had been away, the young bucks from his gang had grown up and got into the booming crack business. Moose and a few of his homies inside still had connections to these young men, so everything was set up for him when he got out. That's why Cliff had come to pick him up.

"Get in, old head, I've come to pick you up."

Moose got into the car, and on the way home, Cliff filled him in on what was happening on the streets. "Yeah, old head, but that gang war shit is played out. Niggas is getting money now. You either hustling, getting high, or you just in the fucking way. We got a tight squad, Moose, and we getting this money. Now we heard all about you coming up. Shit, you was the nigga all of us wanted to be. We know you was the heart of the old gang and that you put in a lot of work. So we need you to be that for us. You see, we doing some nice numbers and niggas be on some hating shit and they be coming at us. We gonna need you to handle them kind of niggas for us. We know you was the shit back in the day. But niggas ain't fist fighting no more, they shooting. Now don't worry about no paper, we going to take care of you on that note. Like I said, we getting this paper. So are you gonna be a part of our team or what?"

Moose didn't hesitate before answering, "Damn right! I ain't got no problem with nothing you just said."

"Okay, Big Moose, you with us now." As Cliff was talking, he pulled up into the King Of Prussia Mall. "What we stopping here for?" Moose asked.

Cliff laughed, "We got to get you some clothes. If you gonna be a part of our team, you can't be wearing that old-ass shit you got on."

The years flew by and Moose had no problems adjusting to his new role. The young bucks helped him out by showing him who was who and how much things had changed since he had been gone. As the enforcer, Moose had no choice but to learn how to shoot. So everyday he was at the gun range until he became proficient enough with firearms. Soon enough, Cliff began to give him assignments, and Moose dealt with whoever needed to be dealt with, no questions asked. Moose became a feared man again. There was a big difference between who he had become and the young man he was before the eleven years in prison. You see, before he went to jail, Moose was known for knockouts. The thing about knockouts is this: you can recover from a knockout. But now Moose was known for taking lives. There is no recovery from a bullet to the head, so the fear that people had was a different kind of fear. It was a mortal fear, the kind that kept you awake at night. Moose had become a ruthless killer and he never left witnesses.

Moose's squad prospered during this time. They were having a ball, enjoying the fruits of their success. Moose had never experienced this kind of success in his life. Moose had plenty of money, his pick of the finest women the city had to offer, jewelry, cars, you name it and Moose had it. He was so consumed in enjoying these fruits that before he knew it, five years had passed and he hadn't sent as much as a postcard to his friends he left back behind Graterford's forty-foot walls. "Fuck it, I don't owe them niggas nothing." Moose had uttered these words one day as he glanced at a picture he and Duck took. Moose took the picture off of his mantle and tossed it into the trash. He wanted no reminders of that time in his life, and just like that, his former friends were forgotten.

"Yo, Moose," hollered Cliff, "we got some work for you. This nigga name Mike. He use to live around here back in the day. This nigga think he can just come back and set up shop. Now I already hollered at him, but the nigga acting like a warning ain't enough. I need you to go see this motherfucker."

"It's done," Moose responded, nodding his head.

Moose went out to see Mike right away. He followed Mike around for weeks, getting to know his habits and to see when he was most vulnerable. During the past five years, Moose had been on top of his game, but lately he had been getting sloppy. Moose started believing his newspaper clippings. He started to believe that he was untouchable. This arrogance caused him to become relaxed, which was a fatal flaw for the kind of work he did.

Shrouded in a blanket of darkness, Moose sat quietly in a stolen car. The corner that he occupied was perfect. He had previously knocked out the streetlight and a big walnut tree blocked out the little light that could reach the corner from the next street light that was a half a block away. Moose's weeks-long surveillance had paid off. He knew that every day at about nine-thirty, Mike left his apartment to collect money from his workers. Moose checked his watch. *Nine-fifteen. Anytime now.* Mike stepped out into the darkness, totally unaware of what was waiting for him outside his home. Moose silently got out the stolen car, pulled out his 9mm, and crept up behind Mike. Just as he was about to shoot, Mike turned around. Mike's eyes opened wide with fear as he stared into the barrel of a gun. Instinctively, he reached for his own gun, but it was too late. At that moment, Moose let off two shots, hitting Mike directly in the forehead. Mike died instantly. Moose was pleased with his work. He smirked while looking over Mike's lifeless body. "Punk motherfucker." Moose chuckled, turned and walked away. Moose got into the stolen car and thought about what he would do for the rest of the night, as if he didn't have a care in the world; but he actually did, because this time he left a witness.

CHAPTER TWENTY-ONE

Rafique had been at Graterford for a little over four years and he could still recall vividly how it was when he first returned from Camp Hill. The hallways were crowded with prisoners. The faint odor of marijuana drifted up Rafique's nose. *What the fuck?* Rafique was amazed at the looseness in the institution. He wasn't exposed to none of this when he was here on the new-side. Rafique stared in wonder; this was nothing like Camp Hill. While at Camp Hill, he was locked in his cell for most of the day and the movement around the jail was very restrictive. Now back at Graterford, Rafique and ten other new admits who were being escorted through the crowded hallway couldn't believe what they were seeing. *Damn, these motherfuckers got on street clothes.* Rafique's head was on a swivel as he responded to shouts of his name. He was surprised at seeing all the familiar faces. In his mind, he always pictured Graterford as being populated by a lot of older-looking strangers, but what he saw instead was all the young guys like himself who had been coming to jail since the juvenile days. As the group continued their walk towards the cell blocks, Rafique spotted his uncles, who at the same time spotted him. His uncles immediately walked up on him. Wease grabbed his box. "What block they got you going to?" Joe-Joe asked him after Rafique finished embracing them.

"I don't know yet," Rafique responded, falling behind the rest of the new admits.

"BZ-9999, you're going to E-Block, so could you please keep up?" The guard had stopped and was waiting for Rafique to catch up.

Rafique picked up his pace.

"That's my block," Wease said.

"Yo, Fique!"

Rafique turned towards the direction that his name was being called from. Walking quickly to catch up was his friend Jody. Jody was one of his friends he grew up with from 52nd Street. Jody had been arrested in 1989 for a homicide and given five-to-ten. Rafique hadn't seen or heard from him since '89.

"What's up, Fique?" Jody said, shaking Rafique's hand. "Yo, I heard about the time you got. That's fucked up, man," Jody continued.

"Yeah, you right about that. It is fucked up. Look, Jody, these are my uncles Joe-Joe, Duck, and Wease. This my man Jody, y'all, I came up with this dude."

All three took turns shaking Jody's hand.

"What block they got you going to?" Jody asked.

"I'm going to E-Block."

"Oh, yeah? That's the block I'm on," Jody said.

"BZ-9999," the C/O called his number again, "you have to report to E-Block, now."

Rafique responded with a nod. As soon as they entered the block, Rafique was taken aback at the size of the block. It was two tiers high and as long as two city blocks.

Hundreds of men, mostly Black and Hispanic, milled around. Some were playing cards on the numerous wooden, picnic-like tables that stretched down the length of the block. Others just walked back and forth. The noise was a steady drone of hundreds of voices speaking at once. Rafique was wide-eyed as he made his way to the guard's station in the middle of the block. Rafique was puzzled by the prisoners behavior. It was as if they had forgotten they were in prison. Rafique turned to Jody. "Why that old head over there got on that old ass sweat suit and them skins."

"Man, some of these dudes be stuck in the time that they got locked up in. So you know he been locked up since the early eighties. That ain't shit, wait until you see the dudes with the bell-bottoms, the big ass afros and the platform shoes."

"Get the fuck out of here. Is you serious?"

"Yeah, I'm serious. Watch, you gonna see them."

Rafique arrived at the guard's station and was assigned to his cell. When he got to the cell, the first thing that he noticed was that the size of the cell, compared to Holmesburg and Camp Hill, was small. It was about the size of a small bathroom. There was a bunkbed on one side, and in the front of the cell was a sink with a toilet connected to it. On the back wall was a rectangular window with bars and filthy screen. There was no one in the cell, so he slid his box under the bed and came back out on the block. "Yo, man, I ain't got no celly," Rafique said to Wease and Jody.

"That won't last long. You'll probably get one tomorrow. So enjoy this shit while it last," Wease said with Jody nodding his head in agreement.

Wease was right, because the next day Rafique had a celly. His name was Brock. Brock was from Southwest

Philly's Bartram Village and he had a life sentence, also. The two of them hit it off immediately. Being in similar situations under similar circumstances makes it easier for two people to bond.

"Ay, Fique, you don't remember me from the streets, do you?"

"Naw, but I don't doubt I met you. I probably was high and just don't remember."

"Yeah, you came down our end to this party. You know Carol Miles, right?"

"Yeah."

"Well, she threw a welcome home party for her brother who did a nine year stint. It was at this bar called the Pub."

"Oh, yeah, I remember that party. You was there that night?"

"Yeah, I was there that night. That's where I remember you from. You had that shit on. Remember when you was arguing with that dude?"

"Yeah, that motherfucker came out of nowhere for no reason and started talking shit. I can't remember what the fuck he said, but I do remember arguing with dude."

"That was me. Well, I mean I siced my homie on you. I ain't gonna lie, I was hating a little bit. You had my jawn all on the dance floor. Plus, all the chicks in the joint was choosing you. You know how it is when a motherfucker from out the neighborhood comes around. So, you know, I told my man to holla at you. If Carol and them ain't step between y'all, it would've been a problem. I had a big ass four pound on me that night."

"Damn, nigga, you was gonna shoot me about a chick?"

"Yeah. Shit, back then I was really in my bag."

"I was strapped, too. So I'm glad shit didn't go no further than a little argument."

"Yeah, me too. Shit, you turned out to be alright."

Brock and Rafique remained cellies for a couple years, but after a while they began to get on each other's nerves. Not because of a particular incident, but because they occupied too small a space for too much time. Imagine you and your best friend spending twelve hours a day, seven days a week locked up in a bathroom together. When either of you has to go to the bathroom or pass gas, the other one has to be there. After a while, even the strongest of bonds will become strained.

Graterford had a deceptive environment. If you weren't careful, you would almost forget that you were in prison. When Mark referred to it as the "Party," no other word would've done it more justice. With the street clothes, the drugs, the freedom of movement, and the looseness of the visits, you could become so distracted that years would have come and gone before you knew it.

In 1995, an event would take place at Graterford Prison that would change the prison for its duration and wake Rafique up to the harsh realities of prison.

A new governor had just been elected to office in Pennsylvania, and one of his major campaign platforms was to clean up Pennsylvania prisons. One of the first things the governor did was appoint new prison administrator. Their mission - clean up Graterford.

The raid came in the evening hours when all the prisoners were locked in their cells for the night. Rafique and Brock were up watching the news.

"Yo, Brock, that's the Ford they talking about. You see that shit?"

A lone reporter could be seen standing outside the prison. As he was reporting, Rafique could see that he was flanked by numerous buses, unloading what appeared to be some type of commando force. There were hundreds of them. "There is a major raid occurring here at Graterford State Penitentiary. I have here at my side the major of the guards who is coordinating this raid …"

"Yo, you see this shit?" Rafique asked, sitting up in the bed with his eyes glued to the television.

"Yeah, this shit crazy."

The night of the raid, everyone in the prison knew that they were coming. So it was no surprise at two o'clock in the morning when Rafique's cell door was snatched open.

"Get the fuck up! Get naked and face the fucking wall!"

Rafique looked up and stared into the face of a guard dressed in all black. He was helmeted and carried a very long nightstick. Rafique and Brock complied, both men got up. Rafique could tell by the glimmer in the guards cold blue eyes that to resist would be a welcoming excuse to cause some physical damage.

"You, big fella, turn around so you can be searched."

Brock did as he was told. Deep wrinkles creased his forehead and his jaw muscles flexed in his cheeks. You could tell that Brock was angry as he went through the humiliating ass-crack search. After the search was over, Brock was allowed to put on his underwear before being handcuffed and removed from the cell.

"Okay, nigger, you're up next."

Rafique swallowed his rage. He understood he was in a unwinnable situation. If he responded in any way he would be beat senseless. Rafique understood that this was what they were trying to get him to do, so he just did as he was told. After he was searched, he was handcuffed and told to stand outside the cell.

The block was full of these guards dressed in black, and Rafique could see the prisoners lined up against the wall all the way down the tier.

"Put your nose up against the wall and don't fucking move," another one of the guards said.

Rafique and Brock stood still with their noses inches away from the wall as the guards ransacked their cell.

"Okay, you monkeys can get back in y'all cage."

Rafique and Brock had their handcuffs removed and they stepped back into their cell. The cell door shut behind them and the two of them just stood and stared. Their cell was a mess. It looked as if a level five tornado had just blown through it. Their personal belongings were mixed up and tossed everywhere. Rafique and Brock looked at one another, and without saying a word, cleared a space off their beds, turned out the lights, and got into bed. Rafique lay on the top bunk wide awake. Tears of rage, helplessness, and humiliation ran freely down his cheeks. It was at that point that he decided that the party was over and he had to do whatever he had to do to get home.

The raid was big news across the state. Politicians lined up in front of the cameras talking about how successful it was. They claimed that they cleaned all the drugs and weapons from the prison and that Graterford would never be what it was. Some of the things they said were just not true. Wherever there was misery there would always be a demand to fill it, and Graterford was filled with misery. Although Graterford became more restrictive, it was still a lot looser than the other prisons across the state.

✫ ✫ ✫

Rafique was abruptly snatched out of his memories by the cell door being open. He looked up, it was his uncle Duck. Rafique could tell by the look on Duck's face that something was wrong. "What's up, Duck?"

"Mike got shot."

"What!"

"Yeah, he got shot last night."

"Is he cool?"

"Naw, man, he gone."

Rafique was silent as Duck's words sank in. He watched his uncle as tears began streaming down Duck's face. Rafique didn't know what to say so he said nothing. Instead, he tried to imagine how Duck felt at losing his only son. He began to think about his cousin Mike and who would want to kill him. It was then that Rafique realized that he wasn't feeling anything. It was as if Duck had just told him a stranger had died. Rafique had felt more grief while watching a sad movie than he felt at hearing about the death of his first cousin. The reason for Rafique's lack of emotion was clear to him. During the whole time he had been incarcerated, he hadn't heard a word from Mike, so in a sense, Mike had become a stranger to him. As he thought about it, he no longer had feelings for people whom he used to be close to but was disconnected from. Rafique shook these thoughts from his mind. "Do you know who shot him?" he asked Duck.

"Yeah, they locked that nigga Moose up for it."

"Moose? Ain't he on parole?"

"Yeah, so he'll be back through here."

"So whatcha wanna do?"

"What? What I wanna do? I can't believe you just asked me that shit. What do you think I want to do? What if it was your daughter that somebody raped or killed? What would you want to do?"

With that said, Duck left Rafique's cell, slamming the door shut behind him, leaving Rafique with nothing but his thoughts.

CHAPTER TWENTY-TWO

Alone again, Rafique contemplated what would happen next. The death of his cousin was having an effect on him that was totally unexpected. He felt himself being pulled into a direction that he was desperately trying to move away from. For the past five years, he had been painstakingly removing the shackles that had imprisoned his mind. How do you discover that you're mentally enslaved when everything around you says that you aren't? For Rafique, the answer to this question was simple: he began to read. As a child, reading was something he loved to do, but as he got older and the streets took hold of his life, reading became something to do only when he had to.

At first, Rafique started out with the Donald Goines-Iceberg Slim-type of books. But when his father sent him the Autobiography of Malcolm X, it opened a whole new world for him. Through reading about the transformation of Malcolm Little to Malcolm X to EL Hajj Malik Shabazz, he began to understand the unique process for black boys to reach manhood. Rafique began to finally understand the struggles of his father trying to save him from a fate that he was now in. These realizations created a thirst for knowledge in Rafique that was unquenchable, so he began to read more. Rafique also began to surround himself with men who were conscious and willing to help a young man find his wings.

One of these older men was Kenyatta. Kenyatta had been down for twenty years and had an extensive library, and he was always trying to share what he knew, especially if you wanted to learn. He took Rafique under his wing and provided him with all the books and reading materials that Rafique's eager mind could handle. Rafique was a fast reader, and before long he had read several of Kenyatta's books: *Breaking The Chains Of Psychological Slavery*, by Naim Akbar; *The Destruction Of Black Civilization*, by Chancelor Williams; *Black On Black Violence*, by Amos Wilson; *The Black Holocaust*, by Del Jones; *Miseducation Of The Negro*, by Carter G. Wilson. After each book Rafique read, he and Kenyatta would discuss the book to make sure that Rafique understood what he was reading and to engage in what Kenyatta called "brain exercising," where the two of them would not only discuss books, but also come up with their own ideas and views. This was important because it taught Rafique how to think for himself, not just parrot something he had read or heard. For Rafique, to have his mind opened up felt as if he had been trapped under a frozen lake with the ice cold water paralyzing his body and his oxygen starved lungs screaming for air. He could feel death near, but at the last minute he's pulled to safety, sucking in life sustaining oxygen. For the first time in his life, he began to really think freely. For the first time in his life, a quote from a poem his father had sent him finally started to make sense. This quote was one of the many things that he discussed with Kenyatta.

"Ay, Kenyatta, my father sent me this quote one time from a poem. It said, uh, 'Stone walls do not a prison make, nor iron bars a cage. Prison is in you mind.' I never really understood what that quote meant until recently," Rafique said as he gazed around Kenyatta's cluttered cell. Books, loose papers, and prison clothing were placed in almost all the available space. Rafique barely had enough room to sit on Kenyatta's bed.

"I've read that poem. As a matter of fact, I got it written down somewhere in here." Kenyatta dug through a stack of papers that were sitting on the floor at the head of his bed. He couldn't find what he was looking for, so he stopped looking. "I could've swore I had that shit right here. I got to get some order to this shit. I got shit everywhere. Anyway, so what do you think it means?"

"Well, to me it means that you can be imprisoned mentally. It means that you can be raised in a way that traps you into a certain way of thinking that you can't get out of. It's like you're brainwashed or something."

Kenyatta nodded his head before responding, "To me, that quote means that people have been socialized to the point where they place limitations on themselves, which hold them back from reaching their full potential. It's like their minds have locks on them that no key can open. So you have people walking around physically free but mentally locked up. You see these walls? That ain't prison. The prison is the restrictions you place upon yourself that won't allow the thinking that's required to regain that physical freedom." Kenyatta paused as he licked the Top Paper he was using to roll up a cigarette. He lit the cigarette and took a deep drag. Kenyatta exhaled the smoke. "Ay, Rafique, you remember how when you were in school… bear with me for a moment. You know how I get when I get going, jumping from one subject to the next. But can you remember when they taught you to believe that Abraham Lincoln was this benevolent man who freed the slaves because it was the morally right thing to do?"

Rafique nodded his head.

"Well, that was some bullshit. The truth was all he did was issue a proclamation saying that all slaves were free in the states that left the union. So in all actuality, he freed no slaves because he had no control over those states. Those states had already formed their own country called the Confederacy. They had their own laws, money, army, and president. It's like me and you having different organizations and I make a statement that everyone in your organization only has to work for three days out of the week. That statement wouldn't mean a goddamn thing to your people because I have no control over them. You follow me?"

Rafique nodded his head again. Kenyatta paused to light his cigarette up because it had burned out. Kenyatta took another drag and exhaled. "Lincoln ain't give a fuck about no slaves. Here, read the part that's highlighted." Kenyatta handed a sheet of paper to Rafique.

> "My paramount objective is to preserve
> The union, not to save or destroy
> Slavery." Abraham Lincoln

After reading the quote, Rafique looked up and Kenyatta continued, "You ever read the 13th Amendment, the one that abolishes slavery?"

Rafique shook his head "no."

"Here it is, read it." Kenyatta handed Rafique another sheet of paper.

THIRTEENTH AMENDMENT
Neither slavery nor involuntary servitude, except as a punishment for a crime whereof the party shall have been duly convicted, shall exist within the United States or any place subject to their jurisdiction.

"You see that, young brother? Slavery was never abolished. The Federal Government was intimately involved in establishing and perpetuating slavery. It passed laws, The Fugitive Slave Act and the Missouri Compromise of 1850, these laws helped further slavery. There was also the Supreme Court decision that bolstered slavery and established segregation, Dred Scott 1857 and Plessy vs. Ferguson 1896. Man, you know once I get going, I can go all day."

"You know, Yatt, I was watching tv the other night and they had on this shit about Thomas Jefferson. Man, they romanticized this story about his raping a slave girl. They made this shit seem like it was a beautiful thing for a slave master to rape a young girl. They called that shit love. I mean they turned this violation into a loving relationship. They failed to mention that she had no choice in the matter. They failed to mention that to a young enslaved girl like Sally Hemmings, Thomas Jefferson, her slave master, was like God. How can you deny God? Here this was one of the authors of the Declaration Of Independence, which says that all men are created equal, yet this motherfucker owned human beings, founding father my ass. I hate when I see black people refer to that rapist as that. They need to tell the story right, this motherfucker was a pedophile. What really fucks me up is, where's the outcry? How come it seems as if I'm the only man that was upset by this? How can you be black and not be angry by the portrayal of the rape of a child as a romantic relationship?"

Kenyatta nodded his head. The rusty-colored dreads that were tied with a piece of string into a ponytail moved up and down his back. He scratched his nappy beard, and a smile stretched his walnut - brown skin and sparkled in his gentle brown eyes as he stared at Rafique. "Rafique, you know what your problem is?"

"My problem? Naw, I ain't know I had one."

"Okay, it's like this. Right now you're a conscious man who understands things because you have been fortunate enough to be made aware. Because of this, your standards have been raised. The problem comes in when you expect other people who haven't been as fortunate as you, in that regard, to see the world as you do. You're talking about people who, like the poem we talked about, have their minds still in chains. You can't hold everyone up to that level, it wouldn't be fair to them. Remember how you use to be, how ignorant you were? You see what happened to you as a result of people judging you in this manner? It wasn't right, was it?"

"Naw."

"So you see, you shouldn't turn around and do the same thing. Once you accept this about people, you won't be so easily frustrated. Alright, check this out, I'm about to change gears again, you know how I get. Let me ask you a question? Who do you hold responsible for your present situation?"

"Who do I hold responsible? Man, I hold myself responsible. Ain't nobody put me in this position but me."

"You think? Well check this out. What you're failing to consider is how much influence played a part in your decision making, and the fact that you were just a child when you were making these choices. Do you know that there are behavioral scientist who study the environmental influences on human behavior? The number one scientist in this field was a cat named B.F. Skinner. Now this cat says that you can delude a people into thinking that they have free will and still control them. Now this ain't some shit that just popped into his head, this was a conclusion after a lot of careful research. So what this means is this: the people that are in control, understanding these things, flood our communities with drugs, guns, and they underfund the public school system.

"By doing these things, they understand that a certain percentage of people will fall victim to the influence that's a direct result of the things that the powers that be put in place. It ain't about knowing right from wrong and choosing to do the right thing as opposed to the wrong thing. It's about being the kind of person that will succumb to the influences. Keep in mind that we're talking about children here. Children who grow up in a society that destroys their sense of self, creating in them a need to look outside themselves for their sense of self-worth. But see, Rafique, you have people out there who understand this and who exploit it. America is eating its kid's Youngblood, just so a few motherfuckers can gain some weight."

These conversations Rafique had with Kenyatta, on top of his studies, produced a man totally alien to the one who walked behind those forty-foot walls all those years ago. This was why Rafique struggled now; he was being pulled into two different directions. His awareness was rebelling against his urge for revenge, to act off emotion. What should he do? Rafique couldn't answer that question right now. Instead, he thought about something his friend Brick was always saying, "Perfection is a moving target." This saying helped Rafique keep things in perspective. All he could do now is live his life the best way that he knew how and continue on his path to maturation.

Because of Rafique's growth, the relationship with his father began to mature as well. Rafique had finally come to a point in his life where he felt comfortable with himself so much so that it transferred to his relationship with his father. The level of communication rose, eliminating a gap that had been in place since he was a small child. The feeling he had now was so natural, it felt as if there was never a circumstance where Rafique didn't feel comfortable with his father.

CHAPTER TWENTY-THREE

IN THE NAME OF ALLAH THE BENEFICENT
THE MERCIFUL
Assallamu Alaikum Wa Rahmatullahi Wa Barakatuh

Rafique,

 I'm waiting here for the subway to show up. I'm on my way to my menial low paying job. I have a lot of concerns about this life I've lived so far. My birthday was last week. Next year this time I'll be a half-century old. I'm responsible for at least seven people coming into this world. I've been a real father to none. At least that's what my children believe. You must determine whether it's true for you. Perhaps that's the reason why you don't write much or keep up your prayers, Allah is the best knower.
 I'm at work now, I'm tired of these spoiled people I have to deal with on a day to day basis for eight hours. Tiredness, frustration, problems, and the pressures they bring will not deter me from writing you this day. I saw the doctor last week, I've got high blood pressure now along with my epilepsy, my liver is

shot and if they keep looking they'll find something else to keep my pressure up and eventually give me a heart attack. I hate doctors. If nothing else makes me sick, they do. I think I'm old before my time. I had so many failures, and disappointments, suffered so many setbacks, missed so many opportunities. In essence I've been what I am, an idealist, a romantic, a black man in white America. I wrote a poem called 'U Don't Know Why I Die.' I've sent you a copy, sometimes I write some good stuff. Interestingly enough people confined wish for freedom in spite of the fact that in a lot of cases they are more free than those who are unconfined walking around. Freedom is a word you write about, argue about, even fight to the death about, but it's still just a word, because men will rob each other of freedom in an effort to obtain their own sense of what freedom is. It's a catch twenty- two, a circular conception of what men mistakenly believe they have a right to, just because they are alive. The problem begins when men attempt to define freedom, other men must lose theirs when that definition is imposed on them.

I assume your doing well as one can, given the circumstances. I ran into one of my Muslim brothers who is an attorney. I explained to him your situation as best as I could. I talked to your mother and I gave her all the information so she could pass it off to you. I hope that he will be of some service. Talk to me Rafique, as ever I love you as I have from your beginnings.

*Love,
Jamil*

TERREL CARTER

U Don't Know Why I Die

I die because of the many roadblocks placed in the path of life's embellishments dead in the face of times trials.
I die because there is no necessity for there to be white victory standing on the back of black tragedy.
I die because you care for your own aggrandizement.
You've made happiness a possession, ruined my concept, killed my inspiration.
I die because Black Life withers in a white dream.
Because god loves, you hate and bemoan your negative fate.
I die because I care, I love, find no room at the inn of my inspiration,
I die because you've turned my women into Black barbie dolls, a thing, a pleasure, my daughters emulate.
My sons love and hate themselves, die young fighting to possess some misbegotten happiness.
You've made happiness a possession, filled my children's hearts with obsession.
My women you take to possess, to protect from me, to provide to my shame, to save face.
I hide behind an image.
You don't know why I die???
I die because my death belongs to me, this you can't take away, cause when I die,

I'M FREE.

Dear Abbee,

I got your letter today and I immediately sat down to respond. I got your message from my mother. She gave me all the information and I called the lawyer. We spoke briefly over the phone. I sent him a copy of the last petition I submitted. He said that he would help. Thanks man, I need all the help I can get.

I believe that we could've been a lot closer than what we were. I don't blame you. although I use to. I've come to understand that life sometimes lays waste to the best of plans so when things happen without a plan, shit can really get crazy. Besides I know I have a mother as well and I know now from dealing with my child's mother, shit ain't never that simple. I'm saying this to say that I hold no more animosity towards you. I also can see how in the past you've reached out to me on numerous occasions. But because of my immaturity, and the fact that I never felt comfortable around you, I could never open up around you. Now though we have an opportunity to make up for wasted years and I intend on making the best out of it.

At this point, I think I'll use this time to try to explain where I'm at with my case, so in the future if you run into someone who can help me you'll be better equipped to explain my situation.

First of all as you know I've been convicted of second degree murder which in this state carries a mandatory sentence of life without parole. In this state founded by Quakers life means just that, life. You get out when you die. I'm presently appealing that decision in hopes of winning a new trial.

The appeal process starts as soon as you are convicted. Before you're sentenced they give you a hearing to determine if you have any issues of illegal practices that you can raise concerning your trial. This is called the Post Verdict Motions. Before you actually get the hearing you have to submit a petition to the court to raise any issues concerning the violations of your rights during trial. Or if you have any new witnesses. I raised several issues at this point.

1) The trial court abused its discretion in approving the defendant to waive the right to a jury and failing to recluse itself.
II) Defendant did not knowingly and intelligently waive his right to a jury trial.
III) Defense counsel was ineffective for advising defendant to waive a jury trial before a judge who had continued and eyewitness probation based on her cooperation against the defendant.
A) Counsel was ineffective for advising defendant not to testify in his own behalf.
B) Counsel was ineffective for the failing to investigate, interview or call any witnesses.

I raised these issues at this hearing, it should have been cut and dry in my favor, but the judge simply denied it. He said some crap about my lawyers trial strategy was not to win the case, but to find me guilty of third degree. That in itself is grounds for an appeal. I never said I did anything. I plead not guilty, furthermore my lawyer was trying to beat the case. What he did was use a diminish capacity defense to fall back on.

Since I've been down I've learned a thing or two about lawyers. First of all he was a court appointed which is different from the Public Defender's Office. Court appointed lawyers have their own practices but are assigned to cases by the state for people who otherwise couldn't afford it. In theory it's a good idea, but in practice as you was able to see it doesn't work. You see, the state pays the attorneys next to nothing. To properly prepare for a homicide it takes lots of money. The measly couple of dollars that the state pays the lawyer is barely enough for an investigator. The state on the other hand has unlimited resources to secure a conviction. So now you have an underpaid lawyer fighting an uphill battle with little resources. Keep in mind that this attorney has other paying clients. So what this does is, it puts your case at the bottom of his *priorities. He spends as little time as possible defending you. This in turn renders him automatically ineffective.*

Anyway after this hearing what's next is called your direct appeal. So when you feel like your constitutional right to a fair trial has been violated and the trial court didn't give you your just do you have thirty days to appeal to the Superior Court, and if that is denied you go to the Supreme Court. At the same time as I was filing the state legislators passed a new law, putting time restraints on the appeal process effectively cutting you off from getting your case reviewed? What happens is this, every time you put something in instead of the prosecution arguing the merits of your issues they just say that you're late, and what that does is it forces you to argue about whether or not you filed on time. They passed this law to deny you your constitutional appellants review and in a draconian measure to speed up executions. Keep in mind while I'm filing these petitions the judges and the courts who are reviewing my case don't do so based on the law as they are mandated, but do so based on their extreme racism which fuels their power to abuse.

I hope I explained things to you good enough, but if there are some things that you don't understand please write back and let me know.

Abbee, I've learned a lot over the years and I'm beginning to see things for what they truly are, as opposed to how they're projected to be. I'm going to close this letter now, so until the next time take care, and know that I love and miss you very much.

P.S.
I liked that poem, I never knew you wrote poetry.
I always wondered where I got it from. I've enclosed a poem I wrote.I hope you like it.

Love,
Rafique

LORD WHAT WAS I THINKING

Lord what was I thinking?
Or was I thinking at all?
A manchild, suffering from a malady
Caught vulnerable and unaware
By the pulse of a city strip.
It beat with a steady rhythm.
A vibration invasion
That penetrated deep within my soul.
Like a moth I was entranced, drawn to the synthetic glow
That corrupted the nighttime skies.
My young eyes were blinded by the glitter of jewels
That rested upon dark flesh
Like the stars sparkling against the backdrop of space.
Walking billboards of fashion designers
Advertising self-esteem.
Was just the medication I needed
To cure this malaise of self - hatred.
Am I good now?
Or am I feeling the ill effects of the "feel good"
The codiene, the pills, the alcohol, the weed.
A young man that flew to close to the sun,
Determind to follow a path to nowhere.
Lord what was I thinking?
Or was I even thinking at all?
Following false trails to manhood
Defined by boys without a clue
As to where that false trail would lead.
All along the way kicking cocaine vials
Like broken off pebbles of cement.
Lord what was I thinking?
Or was I even thinking at all?

Sprouting up through the cracks of concrete
Flowers of womanhood blossomed
Like springtime in a meadow
I picked, I pulled, I uprooted,
Only to own, only to possess.
Not to love, not to admire, not to respect,
Not to protect. But only to conquer as objects of sex.
To lose oneself in pleasures that lasted for just a moment
Then passed by as quickly as a dream,
Leaving behind only death and incarceration,
Ingnorance and shame...
Lord what was I thinking?
Or was I even thinking al all?
Defined and marginalized,
Boxed in and boxed out.
I was the hardest person in the world to know,
A stranger to myself.
Only to discover who I am
At the expense of everything I held dear.
Now my nights are being haunted
By echoes of my ancestors crying out in shame...
"Oh son, what have you done? Couldn't you hear the rattling
Of the chains???
Oh lord what was i thinking?
Or was i even thinking at all???

CHAPTER TWENTY-FOUR

There were times when the confinement and the monotony of being incarcerated nearly drove Rafique out of his mind. During these times, he desperately needed to take his mind outside the prison walls. Sometimes, like a caged lion, he would pace the block back and forth for hours. Other times he would involve himself in some kind of activity like chess, a card game, reading, writing, or just talking to Kenyatta or anything to take his mind off the hopelessness he sometimes felt. At times he would get tired of everything and drop into deep depression where he wouldn't do anything except sit in a dark cell and stare at the walls. This kind of depression would last anywhere from a few minutes to a few days. Usually, to break out of this kind of foul mood he would seek out Kenyatta or any of his select friends and just talk.

"You see, uh, bitches is more emotional than men," said Love, one of the select few and a resident philosopher.

Rafique had just walked up on a conversation Love was having with his other friend Brick.

"Fique, man, Love is over here telling me another one of his fucked up philosophies," Brick said with a smile.

"You see, that there ain't necessary. You ain't got to be saying my, uh, philosophies is fucked up. All I'm trying to say is, uh, bitches is more emotional than men. That's why these women who work in this joint be tripping. So that's why when you put them in a position where they have some control, they go crazy. That's why you can't have one of them bitches being the president. You see, the white man know this, so he do shit to drive motherfuckers crazy. They giving them bitches guns now and sending them off to war, what kind of shit is that? You see, that's why them A-Rabs is so mad. They be like, 'What the fuck! Bitches got guns!' Seeing a bitch with a gun to a A-Rab is like them motherfuckers waking up on the planet of the apes. They be thinking the world coming to an end. That's why they be strapping bombs to their backs." By the time he was finished talking, Love's bald head was glistening with sweat. He leaned against the wall with a serious look on his face. Rafique and Brick were laughing so hard tears were streaming down both their faces. Brick stopped laughing first. "Fique, you agree with that?"

"Ffuuuuccckkk no. You know Love crazy. Men and women are emotional beings. There is a difference, though, and that's men and women are biologically wired and socially conditioned to show different emotions. Men have a chemical in them called testosterone which fuels feelings of aggression and anger. Women, on the other hand, have estrogen which fuels feelings of sadness. Think about it like this, is the woman who cries over a sad movie any more emotional than a man who gets into a fight over a basketball game? They're both showing emotion. It's just that society identifies sadness with emotion more so than anger."

"Now, that there was the dumbest shit I done heard all day. Fique, you bout as smart as a dead flea. Now like I said, women are more emotional than men," Love said.

After standing around listening to Love for a while, Rafique was feeling a lot better. As they continued to go back and forth, Rafique noticed the guard drop a piece of mail in his cell. "Yo, is y'all gonna be out here for a minute? I just seen the guard drop a piece of mail in my cell. I'll be right back." Rafique turned and walked towards his cell.

"Nigga, you know ain't nobody write your motherfucking ass. That there was a return-to-sender jawn that you sent out."

Love got Rafique to laugh one more time before he entered the cell. Rafique looked on the floor and saw the letter. He picked it up, and as he looked at the left-hand corner to see the return address, his nostrils were filled with sweet-smelling fragrance. Where the name should've been, the words "Guess Who" were written. *I wonder who this is?* Rafique wasted no time trying to guess, he ripped open the envelope and began to read the handwritten text.

Dear Rafique,

It took a lot for me to write this letter. I kept thinking after you hung up on me you would call me back or at least write to me. You really hurt me when days turned to weeks and weeks turned to months and months to years, and I got no words from you. The only way I got any information at all was from Pluck. He tried to make me feel better by telling me that he hadn't heard from you either, but that shit didn't help. You were my first love and I really believed that you loved me. But you couldn't have, not how you cut me off. It's been a while now and I don't mean to open up old wounds, but I couldn't write this letter without letting you know how I feel. You know that was, as you would say, some jive shit you did to me. I've been doing okay these past five years. I have two boys now, Rafique and Nazeer. Rafique, I have to tell you this, my oldest is your son. As you can see he has your name. When you first went away I didn't know I was pregnant. When I found out I was trying to wait for you to come back so that I could surprise you with the news. When you called me and told me that you were in jail you didn't give me a chance to tell you. I just knew that you would call me back or at least write me. But you never did, so I started hating you. When I went to the hospital to have our son and you weren't there I hated you even more. You left me out here all alone. I felt like you abandoned me. It took me a long time to get over you and all those negative feelings I had. That's why I haven't attempted to write until now. I just kept telling myself that you didn't want to hear from me.

Little Rafique is five years old now. He looks and acts just like you. Even if I wanted to get you out of my mind I couldn't because I had a constant reminder of you calling me mommy. He knows who you are because I talk about you to him all the time. The older he gets the more he asks of you. This is why I finally decided to write. It's time for you to meet your twin. Rafique, please don't be mad at me. If you think about it you're partly responsible. I'm sorry for the part I played in it, could you please forgive me?

I got on with my life as you told me to. Although I waited around for you to get at me for like two years. When you didn't I just gave up hope that I would ever hear from you again. I met this guy who in the beginning treated me well. After about a year I got pregnant. After I gave birth to Nazeer, shit just changed. He started abusing me physically and mentally. He showed me no respect at all. I know that I should leave him but, I just can't seem to do it. He tells me I'm ugly and if it wasn't for him nobody would want me. I started thinking maybe that's why you cut me off. Rafique tell me that ain't the case. My life now is stuck it ain't going nowhere. I keep telling myself that I need to go back to school, but this nigga just keep on discouraging me. I just be so depressed I don't feel like doing nothing. I know you got your own problems and I'm sorry for beating you in the head with this. So I'm going to sign off now. So take care baby and know that I'll always love you no matter what.

Love Aisha

P.S.
Here's my mother's address:
4901 First Street N.W., Apt. D, Washington DC 20011
Write back soon!!!

Rafique put the letter down. His heart throbbed with regret. He had safely tucked away thoughts of Aisha a long time ago, but reading her words brought back her presence as if she was never gone. Rafique's hand trembled slightly with anticipation as he grabbed his pen. He had been living with this regret and beating himself up for years for letting her go. Now his only hope was that she could truly forgive him so that he could renew their relationship and meet his son. Rafique began to move the pen across the page.

Dear Aisha,

I pray that on the arrival of this letter, you and yours are under God's protection, and that you are having things your way. I pray that your health is well both mentally and physically and I hope that this could be the start of something that was never meant to end. As for myself, I'm good you know, just trying to make the best out of a very fucked up situation.

When I entered the cell and I saw this letter on the floor with no name on it, I thought to myself who could this be? Once I began to read it I realized that it was you. To be honest, I was very glad you wrote me. Aisha, I've been away now for five years, and every day of that time I've spent thinking of you and how much I miss you. Before I continue I have to apologize. I'm sorry I hurt you and if I could do things different I would. I was being selfish at the time. I was so concerned about myself and my feelings I never took the time to consider yours. I should've never handled things the way I did, but you have to understand my mindset at the time. I thought I was making it easier for you. I see how foolish I was then. First of all I had no right to tell you not to support me. That was a decision you needed to make.

Aisha, since I've been old enough to have children I always wanted a son. Now don't get me wrong, having my daughter was one of, if not the best thing that has ever happened for me. I still wanted a son though. I'm at a loss for words, I'm stuck. As I was reading your letter my heart pace picked up when I read I had a son. Thank you for telling me. I'm not upset with you. That would be a waste of energy. Besides, I owe you an apology, I left you out there. I was the one who cut you off. I'm responsible for what has happened to us, not you. You have nothing to be sorry about. Getting this news has made things even more urgent with me as far as getting the fuck out of here. In the meantime you have to bring him up here. Plus, I would love to see you. I'm feeling all kinds of shit right now. Happiness for the obvious reasons, and sadness because I've already missed five years of his life.

TERREL CARTER

Before I bring this letter to its close, I have to mention a few things. I'm sorry to hear that you're in the relationship that you're in. I know that your boyfriend has to be out of his mind. As I read your letter it upset me that this clown who probably professes his love for you could at the same time treat you as he does. I know that he doesn't understand how important you are therefore he takes you for granted. He doesn't understand that you're supposed to love, respect, and protect your woman, the mother of your child. What's really fucking me up is you though. Damn, Eesh, from what I can see from your letter your self-esteem is shot. Eesh, your self-esteem is your core of personal beliefs. What happens when you have low self-esteem is this, the core of your personal beliefs come from messages. Constant exposure to these messages causes you to internalize them. Once that occurs they become beliefs. Now if the messages you're taking in are negative over a period of time you will develop a negative sense of self-worth. In other words when that chump tells you that nobody wants you but him, you start believing that nut shit. So much so that you would ask me if I feel that way about you. Eesh you are the most beautiful girl I ever had in my life. But what I say don't matter if you don't believe it.

Eesh, what you need to do now is start telling yourself that you are beautiful and that you are worthwhile. I know that you're probably thinking that to do this won't be too difficult, but it ain't as easy as it seems. The reality is, that it's kind of complex. The complexity is not in saying these things it's in believing them. So, baby examine your beliefs about yourself and whatever you have in your life that ain't for the success of Aisha, cut it the fuck off. Aisha, I know it can be difficult to move on, but you have to. You see, the most important person in the world is you. If you ain't cool then those that depend on you ain't cool either. It's all about you. Keep in mind that it's very important for you to think highly of yourself for your sense of *self - worth because at any time a person can make you feel like shit if they have that kind of power over you. I know things can be rough but I know you, and I know that you are a strong sister, and if anybody can pull through this shit, you can. Baby life is full of ups and downs, character is built on how you handle the shit that comes your way. Don't be afraid to be by yourself, even though it may hurt, you got to stand strong.*

So in closing I pray that my words can be a source of inspiration, encouragement, and strength. So until pen meets paper, take care, and be careful.

P.S.
I put a little something extra in this letter I hope you like it.

Love,
Rafique

MY DREAM

I saw her in a silk dress holding a white rose...
She smiled, looked me up and down, and raised it to her nose...
For a tick, I was nervous, but I got my nerve up finally...
She said, "I've seen you before, I know who you are, of you people speak highly...
I stood in shock, contemplating the words she spoke...
She continued, "I know you need a woman, to ride, to give hope, so I'm with you to the wheels fall off, forever or for broke...
I took a deep breath, extended my hands to hold hers in my palms...
She said, "All that I ask is that you never give up, and I'll be with you, support you, you know the whole nine...
I watched her in awe while she walked away as dimness enveloped the scene...
I kept wondering, who is this woman who haunts my dreams...
Before she completely faded I yelled, "Where can I find you???"
Her voice echoed back, "I'll be where you need me to be!"
Then she was gone, like a puff of smoke, vanished from my view...
A ghost of an image was all I had as my eyes combed the scene....
Then I heard the lock to this cell click, and it woke me from MY DREAM
The next night I dreamed again, and I realized that Eesh, you were the one...
Lips soft as rose petals, skin French - Kissed by the sun...
On a white sand beach, snaring intimate thoughts, holding hands...
Creating a scene that writers describe, as our feet left tracks in the sand...
The warmth of the sun caressing our skin...

The roar of the ocean, the cries of the gulls, was the background din...
We stopped in our tracks as nature's melodies united our souls...
We became lost in each others gazes and our passions rose...
Our bodies moved closer, no time to think, no time to react...
But just before our lips met, I woke up and shed a tear,

CAUSE I REALIZED WHERE I WAS AT.

CHAPTER TWENTY-FIVE

The digital alarm clock read 4:30 a.m. The annoying beep rang continuously in her ear. Sleepily, she looked over at the red numbers glowing in the darkness of her bedroom. She reached out and fumbled with the clock, trying to find the button to make the beeping stop. Finally, she located the button and turned the alarm off.

No matter how early she went to bed, it was something about getting up at four in the morning that didn't allow her to feel completely rested. She yawned. *Damn, I really don't feel like going to this motherfucker today.*

Monique Thompson hated her job. She worked for the Pennsylvania Department of Corrections at the all-male Graterford State Penitentiary. Her job depressed her. When Monique stepped inside those walls, she entered a world all unto itself. It was a world full of wasted potential, shattered dreams, and misery. A world that was full of black men, young, old and mostly poor. She had her preconceived perception of what life was like behind those walls from the TV shows, movies, what she heard in the neighborhood, and what they told her at the training academy. The reality was far different from what she believed.

In Monique's first few weeks at work, she began to get a different perspective. She saw that these men who were convicted of some horrible crimes, vilified and dehumanized, were still just men. She began to see that these men were no different than her brothers, her father, and her lovers. There were men she knew, men that she grew up with, and men that she would get to know. So after a while, she realized that all of her preconceptions, although they had some basis in truth, were greatly exaggerated. It became very hard for Monique to remain professional and to maintain the code of ethics that all correctional employees are expected to maintain.

One of the main reasons why it was so hard for her to maintain was this: Monique was twenty-seven years old and at her sexual peak. She worked around thousands of men of all shapes and sizes. Some of these men were brilliant and had the ability to stimulate her mentally in a way that had never been done before. There were men who were smooth and always knew exactly what to say, and men who were built like Greek gods and some of the most handsome men she had ever seen in her life. This is what made it so hard. It was only natural to be attracted to at least a few of them. Monique fought with herself constantly, because to become involved with a prisoner was a major security breach and cause for immediate termination. Monique needed her job. She was a single mother raising three children with only a high school diploma. This was a good wage-paying job with benefits, which she desperately needed for her children. To be responsible or to give in to your natural desires was a timeless battle of the self that would last as long as Monique remained at her job.

Monique got out of the bed and slowly walked to the bathroom. She turned on the shower, took off her panties and bra, and stepped into the steaming hot water.

The shower water was nice and hot and the steam filled the confines of the bathroom. Monique closed her eyes and let the force of the water relax her tension-filled muscles. As she applied a soapy lather to her body, Monique found herself thinking about one prisoner in particular, Rafique. He was so damn fine, nice and chocolate just like she liked her men. She became sexually aroused as she pictured him standing in the shower with her. She became moist, not just from the water, as she reached down and begin to lightly touch herself. Monique sucked her teeth and removed her hand. She was a bit ashamed at her lack of self-control. She bit her thick bottom lip out of frustration. With Rafique still on her mind, she began to think about the day she first saw him walking through Graterford's gloomy corridors. *I know him from somewhere, but I can't remember from where. He just a baby, though. Shit, he probably ain't ready for all this anyway.* Monique could recall clearly how after that day she began to watch him, seeing how he carried himself and who he dealt with. She then began to discreetly ask around about him. Her questions turned up the fact that he wasn't as young as he appeared. He was actually older than she was, he just had a baby face. After satisfying her reservations, she decided that she would spark a conversation with him just to see where his head was at. This was Monique's mind-set as the shower water cascaded down her body. *Next time I see him I'ma say something to him. Let me get the hell out of this shower. I'm in here bullshitting and I'ma fuck around and be late for work.*

"Main yard!" the C/O hollered out. His voice echoed up and down the cellblock. It was one o'clock in the afternoon and time for the main yard. Rafique left out the cell to get some fresh air and sun.

Rafique found a quiet spot in the corner of the yard, sat down on the concrete bench, and began to relax, watching a couple of guys practicing their batting techniques. After a while his mind began to drift, and he started thinking about what he needed to do to in order to regain his freedom. As he racked his brain for ideas, his thoughts were interrupted by a woman's voice.

"What's up, Rafique?"

It was C/O M. Thompson, the same Thompson that Rafique encountered when he first came upstate. She had been patrolling the yard and spotted Rafique sitting by himself. She was bored, and already having made up her mind to step to him, she saw that this was a perfect opportunity to do so.

Rafique stared at her. She looked good with her knees locked back and her chocolate skin glistening with sweat. "What's up, Ms. Thompson?"

Monique stared back at him and smiled as her heart pounded in her chest. "Why you ain't working out?"

"I will. I just wanted to enjoy this sunshine for a minute."

For a while, the conversation was general as they talked about a little bit of everything. Rafique knew that the general conversation was a prelude to something else. What it was, he didn't know, but he was about to find out. So he began to turn the heat up. "Ay, Ms. Thompson, do you mind if I ask you something personal?" Rafique had to be careful now. Ms. Thompson was still the police and could go into cop mode at any moment.

"Yeah."

"What kind of men are you attracted to?"

"I'm not going to answer that question because I don't want to incriminate myself."

That was the answer he was looking for. But he was still cautious, so instead of jumping right in, he probed some more. "Being attracted to someone ain't a crime. That's a natural thing between men and women."

"Yeah, well, this ain't a natural place and I don't trust nothing about it to answer a question like that."

"Okay, I can respect that. Having the position that you have and not really knowing me like that, I can see why you answered it like you did. Look, I got to go get me some pull-ups in before they call the yard in. It was real nice talking to you, though. It ain't every day that I get to be blessed with the presence of someone as fine as you."

Monique blushed. "Thanks for the compliment, and to answer your question about what kind of men I'm attracted to, fine ones. And you is a cutey pie."

It was Rafique's turn to smile as he stood up and walked away to the pull-up bar. *The door is open now. Next time I see her I'm going at her.*

A few days later Rafique would get his opportunity. Ms. Thompson was working his block. Rafique saw her as soon as she walked on the block. *Damn, there she go right there. I'm going at her today.* Rafique approached her. Monique saw him and smiled. "Ms. Thompson, you got a minute? I need to holla at you."

"Yeah, I got a minute. What's up?"

"Look, I don't know if you know this or not, but I got a thing for you. Now if I'm overstepping my bounds, let me know now and I'll fall back."

"You alright. And, no, I ain't know you was feeling me."

"Okay, it's like this, now that you know that I'm feeling you, the next logical thing would be for me to find out if the feeling is mutual?"

"Yeah, you alright."

"Okay, now the next step is for me to try to get to know you. You see, I learned a long time ago that it's the knowledge of a thing that allows you to possess that thing. I'm saying that to say I'm trying to know you in order to have you."

Monique smiled and nodded her head as Rafique kept talking. "I know you got a big-ass fan club around here, and dudes be constantly coming at you. I ain't trying to be one of your fans. I need for you to separate me from the rest. Let me take that back. You ain't got to separate me, I'ma separate myself."

"How you planning on doing that?"

"Once you get to know me, you'll see that I ain't like no other man you met or gonna meet. It's only one of me in this world and before long you gonna be mine. That's what's gonna separate me from everyone else. You gonna be claiming me as your man."

"I see you ain't lacking in confidence."

"That's because I'm used to getting what I want, and in order to achieve this I understand that if you don't stand up, you won't be seen. If you don't speak up, you won't be heard. And right now I want you. How you gonna see me if I don't stand up? How you gonna hear me if I don't speak up?"

"When you gettin out?"

"You know what, ordinarily I would lie and tell you a couple years. But something about you is telling me I don't have to lie. I got a life sentence."

At hearing those words, Monique's heart dropped. She knew what having a life sentence meant. "You got life?"

"Yeah."

Monique was silent as what she learned sank in.

Rafique spoke quickly, not wanting her to think too much. "Look, Ms. Thompson, we just got to take this thing real slow. For now, I ain't looking for no love connection or nothing like that. I'm just looking for a friend, and when I get out it can go wherever you want it to go. I need for you to believe that I'm getting out, though, or it'll be hard for you to be the friend I need you to be."

"Do you believe you're getting out?"

"Absolutely, with every fiber of my being."

"Well, if you believe you're coming home, I'll believe it, too."

Rafique looked at her name tag. "What does the M stand for?'

"Monique."

"Do you mind if I call you that?"

"No, I don't mind."

"Alright, Monique, like I said, I really want to get to know you. I mean everything that makes Monique who she is I want to know. It ain't gonna be one way either, because at the same time I'ma give you the same opportunity to get to know me as well. Don't think that all of what I'm saying is about getting some. Don't get me wrong, though, 'cause if the opportunity knocks I'd be a fool to not answer. It's just that what I need right now is more than just physical. Although I miss the physical shit, I miss the small things more. You know, all the things that I use to take for granted. Like right now just hearing your voice is a treat for me. It's like when you smoke a joint and you favorite song come on. You close your eyes and say to yourself, this my song, and it seems like the music becomes a part of you as it flows through your body. You know the feeling I'm talking about?"

Monique nodded her head as Rafique kept talking.

"Well, that's what I'm feeling when I hear your voice. You see, all day long all I hear is deep-ass voices. I've been deprived of all things feminine and as a result of that, I've developed a deep appreciation for that femininity that's been missing in my life. So all those things about women I used to take for granted are the things I miss the most."

"Rafique, like I said, I'm with all that you saying, but it's gonna be real hard because of the circumstances."

"Monique, nothing worthwhile comes easy. The harder a thing is to obtain, the more it'll be appreciated. Look, I just had to get all that off my chest, and from your reaction, I'm glad I did. Monique, you don't remember me do you?"

"You know what? When I first saw you, your face did look real familiar. I was beating myself up trying to remember where I knew you from."

Rafique chuckled. "When I first came upstate you was down in assessment. You asked me was I locked up for killing someone black or white. Then you asked me where I want my body sent. That shit stuck with me. If I wouldn't have seen you for another ten years, I would have remembered you."

"That's where I remember you from. I remember now. Yeah, see, I can count on one hand how many times I been down assessment. That's why your face looked so familiar. That was a few years ago, wasn't it?"

"Yeah, it was five years ago to be exact."

"I remember that day clearly now, I was like, look at this little young boy. Then I saw your paperwork and saw how much time you had and was like, damn. That's why I said what I said. I was trying to make you feel better. The thing about your body, well that was part of the job."

"Look, Monique, I ain't trying to hold you hostage no longer. Plus, the way these motherfuckers keep peeking over here, you would think they could read lips. So I'ma bounce for now, but you know we'll talk soon." Rafique gave her a wink, turned, and walked away.

Over the next few months, Rafique and Monique became close. They established a friendship without compromising her job. They just planned for the time when he would regain his freedom and what part they would play in each other's lives.

CHAPTER TWENTY-SIX

Around the time Rafique was getting cool with Monique, Aisha resurfaced in his life. Aisha had received Rafique's letter, and soon after that she made the trip to Philly, bringing along his son.

Rafique stepped out into the visiting room and glanced around. The room was jam-packed full of brown faces. A low murmur of voices permeated the room. Every once in a while a snatch of a phrase or a word or two became distinguishable from the undertone. The paint on the walls was a drab beige color, contributing to a subtly subdued atmosphere as if happiness was being smothered by a blanket of suppression. Rafique was nervous. Anticipating the first meeting felt as if a hundred needles were sticking him in the gut. Finally, she descended down the stairs and entered the room. Rafique was so focused on her presence that all the noise and all the sights had faded away, leaving nothing but Aisha and the little boy that trailed behind her. The beating of Rafique's heart had reached a crescendo when she spotted him and smiled.

Aisha looked exactly the same since the last time he saw her, beautiful. She had picked up a little weight, but it just enhanced her beauty. His son, well, he looked like a miniature version of himself, from the complexion to the eyes to the small cleft in his chin. For Rafique, looking at his son was like looking at a picture of himself when he was a small child. Rafique walked over and greeted them as tears slowly leaked down from his eyes. He gave Aisha a warm hug, and as he relished the softness of her body, he whispered into her ear, " I missed you so much."

"I missed you, too, baby," Aisha said as she kissed him lightly on the neck.

"Step back and let me look at you, girl. Damn, you look good. You haven't changed a bit."

Aisha did a pirouette. "Thank You."

Rafique looked at his son, who stared back at him, eyes wide with wonderment. "What's up little man?" Rafique said as he picked him up and kissed him on the cheek. "Do you know who I am?"

"Yeah, you my dad."

"That's right, I'm your dad." Rafique laughed as he put his son down. He then led them to their seats.

Little Rafique was little shy at first, but as the day wore on he began to loosen up. They played for hours as Rafique tried to mike up for the past five years in a few short hours.

"Can you fight?" Rafique asked his son.

"Yeah, I can fight."

"Oh, yeah? Well let me see how you hold your hands."

Little Rafique held his hands up just like Rafique thought he would, like his mother showed him how.

"That's good, little man, but let me show you something. First of all, tuck your chin. Yeah, like that. Now hold your elbows closer to your body, bend your knees a little…yeah, that's it. Now snap that left hand out…no, your other left. Yeah, like that. Now when you get home, I want you to practice what I've shown you. The next time you come to see me, I'ma show you something else."

Aisha looked on with a proud look on her face, not saying a word. The expression she wore looked as if everything she ever wanted was just in the space she now occupied as she watched the two men that she loved interact. Three hours into the visit, Little Rafique climbed into his father's lap and went to sleep. At this time, Rafique turned to Aisha, "Thank you, baby, for bringing my son to me. If you was a fucked up kind of person, I could've lived my whole life never knowing that I had a son."

"Rafique, you don't have to thank me for this. I couldn't live with myself if I didn't allow our son to meet his dad. Looking at you two today playing and just enjoying each other's company was all the thanks I'll ever need."

Rafique and Aisha talked as their son slept. They talked of old times, the present, and the future. Aisha let him know that she was able to get out of the hurtful relationship that she was in, and she thanked him for helping her. She let him know that she had gotten back into school and that she was working. "Rafique, it's kind of hard, but you letters of encouragement kept me focused. I just wish you were home so that we could be a family. Until that day comes, though, I'ma be right here with you, riding this thing out 'til the wheels fall off."

"Aisha, I have to let you know, riding this thing out ain't gonna be easy. There will be times when you're just gonna need me out there physically, and when I'm not and you get frustrated, then what? Are you gonna drop out of my life?"

"To be honest, I don't know what I'll do. I know what I won't do, though, and that's drop out of your life. I'ma be right here doing this thing with you for better or for worse. It's gonna take a little more than time to chase me away."

The visiting hours ended at three o'clock. Little Rafique awoke at two-thirty, and for the last half hour of the visit all three of them talked. The flicking of the lights meant the visiting time was up. Little Rafique looked his father in the eye. "Dad, I want to stay with you."

"You can't, little man, but your mom will bring you back up here soon."

Little Rafique wasn't trying to hear that as tears flowed from his eyes. Rafique picked his son up and placed a kiss on his forehead as Little Rafique tightly wrapped his little arms around his father's neck. Rafique tried to comfort him, but his son wouldn't stop crying.

Aisha looked on with tears of her own flowing freely down the sides of her face. Finally, she took their boy, promising him that she would bring him back soon. Little Rafique kept crying. Aisha put her son down and walked into his father's arms. "Baby, I'll be back. I'ma come up at least twice a month. Don't worry, I'm here now, baby, and I promise you that I'll never leave. She kissed Rafique passionately for a few seconds until, reluctantly, she pulled away, turned, and left the visiting room.

CHAPTER TWENTY-SEVEN

SUMMER 1999

Two more years had passed, bringing the total amount of years Rafique had been incarcerated to seven. Nothing had changed for him on his appeals so far. In fact, getting a life sentence overturned in Pennsylvania was rare, and so far it's been no different for Rafique. It's just been rejection after rejection. Most men in similar positions had just resigned themselves to living out the remainder of their lives behind those concrete and steel, forty-foot walls. Although at times Rafique felt like his situation was hopeless, he still fought hard. He refused to let his burning desire for freedom become extinguished. Every waking moment Rafique battled the insidious thought that he'd grow old and die in the penitentiary. It was a battle that Rafique had vowed to win. All he needed was that one chance that would lead to his freedom.

That break would come to him one day when he was least expecting it. It happened one day as he was walking the yard.

"Yo, Fique."

Rafique turned towards the direction that he heard his name being called. He squinted his eyes to get a clear picture of the man who was calling him. The closer he got, the clearer the man became. It was Buff.

"Damn, what's up, Buff?"

"What's up, Fique? Damn, man, I ain't seen you since the night you got locked up."

"I know, man, it's been a long time."

"I know. It's been almost ten years. How you been holding up?"

"I've been maintaining, you know, keeping my head above water. I ain't gonna hold you, it's been rough, man, but I ain't gave up yet."

"How's your case coming along? Are you still in court?"

"Yeah, I'm still in court, but they keep on shooting my shit down."

"Fique, why didn't you use me as a witness? I was there with you that night, remember? Fuzz asked me to go with him first."

"Buff, the last thing I remember about that night is taking those fucking Dumb-Dumbs I got from Tash. What happened after that?"

"About an hour after you got those pills, Fuzz came up and asked us did we want to go get some paper. Ain't nobody want to go, so he just stepped."

"Damn, Buff, where you been all these years? I could've used you."

"Man, ain't nobody ever ask me shit. I would've said something."

"Are you willing to testify now?"

"Are you serious? Fucking right! They got you doing a life bid for some shit you ain't even do."

"Okay, look, I need you to go to the law library and tell one of the brothers there that you need an affidavit typed up. Once you get it typed up, you got to go to the notary, that's at one o'clock. Just go to the guard on the block and tell him you need a pass to the notary. When you get the pass, bring the statement around with you and I'll meet you there. We can do this tomorrow 'cause it's too late to do it today."

Buff and Rafique talked for the remainder of the yard period. Buff informed Rafique how he got a three-year bid for cocaine possession, got out, and stayed cool for a while before he violated his parole, which brought him back. After the yard was called in, they shook hands and went back to their respective blocks.

When Rafique got back to his cell, he was brimming with excitement. This was the break he was looking for. He was so excited he didn't notice the letter on the floor until almost an hour later. He picked the letter up and saw that it was addressed from his daughter.

Dear Dad,

I'm writing this letter because I'm feeling alone. Dad I need you out here with me. Right now in this time of my life I'm going through some changes and I really need your help. Dad I love you and I want you to come home and be with me now. I would hope on Father's day you'll be home and I'm at your house and I make you breakfast. Dad I'm messing up real bad. I had sex with an eighteen year old boy and didn't use protection. I skipped school, I don't know what's wrong with me at all, it's like I don't care anymore. I just want you to come home and be with me to help me through this. I just feel like giving up. I just want to say fuck it. I know it's wrong for me to have unprotected sex and to skip school. I just really need you to help me. I want you to be there on my graduation day from high school. I want you to come home and get me and we just go away. I'm so scared. I just feel like running away from it all and never coming back. Dad I love you and I miss you. So I'm just going to bring this letter to a close telling you to pray for me and be strong for me. Dad I love you and I'll always be there no matter what. I'm praying every night that you come home to me so that me and you can be a happy family.

Love your daughter,
Shante

TERREL CARTER

Dear Shante,

How's my baby girl? I pray that you and the family are under God's protection and that everything is well. I received your letter today and as I finished reading it, it made my quest for freedom more urgent. Shante, I understand what you're going through, you see, believe it or not it wasn't that long ago that I was a teenager, so I can still remember how I felt. Right now you have an advantage, which is a very close relationship with your father. When I was younger I wasn't close with my mother or father so what that meant was the only advice that I would listen to came from my friends and they were just as dumb as I was. It was the blind leading the blind. So right now I'm a little disappointed with you. Not because you're making mistakes, but because you're making mistakes that you don't have to make. Shante, you have to take advantage of the relationship that we have. That's what I'm here for, to guide you, to help you avoid the mistakes that your mother and I made. Take heed to the things that I tell you, it's for your own good. I'm trying to give you the game baby girl, so you can be one step ahead of everyone else.

Shante, to give yourself to someone is a big step. I know that you're not looking at it in this manner. You think that you may love someone or that the guy will love you if you have sex with him. But let me put it to you like this. Say like you had a million dollars. Now would you give this guy the whole million, not some of it, not half, but all of it. Not keeping a dime for yourself. I know that your answer to this is no. And if that's the case then how could you give him yourself. Aren't you worth more than a million dollars? You see, baby girl you have to start loving yourself. Because if you love yourself you will value yourself a whole lot more than you do. Think about someone that you love, someone that no matter what they do you still love them. Think of your mother and what if anything you would give your mother up for. Think about the love that won't allow you to give up your mother for nothing in the world. Now do you feel that way about yourself? You need to be honest with yourself when you answer this question, and if you are honest then you'll see that I'm right and that you need to start telling yourself that you love you. Say this every day and you'll begin to see how it will affect your life immediately.

Shante, I know you need me out there, and I want to be there with you more than anything in this world. The reality is I'm not. So what are you going to do? Are you just going to say fuck it and stop using your ability to think? If you really want me out there you have to put yourself in a position to be able to help me. You may be the person that helps me regain my freedom. You can't do that by cutting school and setting yourself to be a teenaged mother or worse, becoming infected with the AIDS virus. Shante, you're soon to be fifteen. Your main concern should be your future. Once your goals are secured, then you can play. Now I can sit here and write until my fingers hurt, but it won't mean a thing unless you trust me, and do what needs to be done.

We've come a long way and I'm glad that we are as close as we are, because it wasn't that long ago that we weren't. I know sometimes it may seem that I'm angry with you, but that's only because I love you and I want the best for you, and I want you to want the same. So when you settle for less it disappoints me. One day soon if God is willing I'll be out there again and when that day comes it's gonna be me and you. I'm bringing this letter to it's close and in doing so express my unconditional love. I love you Shante and I miss you very, very much.

Love your father,
Rafique

Rafique folded the letter up, put it in an envelope, and addressed it to his daughter as the call for count rang up and down the cellblock. As Rafique lay on his bunk, all he could think of was his daughter and the new witness he had.

When count cleared, he went to the phone to call his mother to let her know about the witness and to call his daughter to make sure her trip to DC went okay. He had finally arranged for her to meet her family out there.

Rafique picked up the phone and dialed his mother first. His mother picked up after a couple rings. A recording came on: "You have a collect call from inmate, 'Rafique,' at the State Correctional Institute at Graterford. Custom-calling features are not allowed during this call. This call may be monitored and or recorded. To refuse this call, please hang up now, to accept this call, please press one."

Tonya pressed the one, accepting the call.

"You may proceed with your call, thank you."

"Hello, Mom?"

"Hey, Rafique, how are you?"

"I'm cool, I got some good news."

"What's going on?"

"Well, I ran into this guy that was there the night that this case happened. He told me I never went with the guy Fuzz. He said Fuzz left by himself. And he said that he was willing to testify for me."

"Oh my God, Rafique, that's wonderful. So now what?"

"Well, he's getting an affidavit together now. As soon as that's done, I'll put a petition in for a new trial. Mom, this is the break I been looking for. If everything goes right I'll be able to get out of here."

Rafique talked to his mother for a few more minutes before hanging up to call his daughter.

☆ ☆ ☆

Shante sat in her cluttered bedroom surveying the mess. Clothes were strewn everywhere, along with books and papers from a book report she had just completed. The walls of her room were adorned with posters of Tupac Shakur. She loved Tupac. She believed that he was the greatest rapper ever.

I need to clean my room up before my mom gets home bitching. Shante got off the bed, went to her dresser drawer, and picked up the picture of her father. It was the picture that she took the last time she visited him a couple weeks ago. *I look just like my Dad. Damn, I wish he was home, then we both could've gone to DC so that I could meet my family down there.* As thoughts of her father floated through her mind, Shante began to think back to when she was younger and how much their relationship had grown since then.

As far back as she could remember there was always a darkness over the person she resembled the most, her father. Shante knew who he was and his name was Rafique, but that was the extent of her knowledge. That sacred bond between father and daughter didn't exist for them back then.

Shante had very few memories of her father before he was arrested and went to prison with a life sentence. That was mainly because of his immaturity. You see, Rafique was but a child himself when she was born. As a result of his immaturity, the streets became more important to him than spending time with his child. That caused their relationship to suffer greatly. Rafique was aware that something wasn't right because she would cry every time he would come around. But Rafique just attributed that to her just being a baby. He figured that once she got older she would grow out of it. Rafique believed he had plenty of time to turn the situation around, but he had no idea that he would end up in jail and the time he thought he had would no longer exist.

Shante, in the meantime, resented him for going to jail. She hated when people looked at her funny because her father was a jailbird. All the blame was heaped on her father, and the dislike grew. Shante hated going to see him in jail, so she would just ignore him when she was forced to go.

As Shante got older her views began to change. Although she gave her father the cold shoulder, that didn't stop him from reaching out to her. As a result of his persistence and the fact that her grandmother made sure that she came to see him twice a month, she became more and more comfortable around him and her anger subsided. Shante began to feel a need for this man in her life, so little by little she began to open up.

By the time she was thirteen and entering high school, Shante was in trouble. Adolescence had kicked in. With her body bursting with hormones, she found herself in situations where the advice and love of her father would have served her well. Puppy love hit her hard, and Shante became involved with an older boy who convinced her of his love. He convinced her that the only way to express that love was through sex. So at the tender age of thirteen, she lost the most precious thing that a woman has, her virginity, and she let it go for a lie. Shante would soon realize this after the deed was done and the boy stopped calling. She was devastated. During this time her grades began to reflect her state of mind and it was easily noticeable. Her mother immediately tried to put the hammer down, but that made Shante rebel. She started being disrespectful towards her mother and that caused their relationship to fracture.

So many things were happening at once. So many things were bouncing around in her young mind and there was no one in whom she felt that she could confide in. One day it all came to a head when, out of nowhere she began to cry. Shante cried hard and she couldn't stop. At that moment she needed her father and he wasn't there. God must have heard her cries because in the middle of her mini breakdown, the phone rang. It was father. At that moment Shante let her defenses down completely and revealed everything to her father. It was then that the wall separating them came crumbling down and that sacred bond that they had been missing was formed.

Almost like magic, Shante had a new best friend. She began to write to him and share her innermost thoughts and dreams. Her father would respond, not with criticism but with encouragement, love, and fatherly advice. He encouraged her to think and question the things that she didn't understand or that didn't make sense, no matter where the information came from. Her father began to talk to her about boys and the games they played. He talked to her about racism, politics, and the injustices of the criminal justice system. These discussions, along with the fact that she wanted him home, piqued her interest in the law, so much so that she wanted to become a lawyer. Although her father didn't know it, he inspired Shante to excel in everything she did.

Shante was no longer ashamed of this man, and their love was stronger than it had ever been. She felt blessed to have him for a father, and she thanked God for him everyday.

Shante placed the picture back on top of her dresser and began to straighten up her room. She needed to get it done because her mother would be home any minute. As she began picking up her clothes, the phone rang.

✤ ✤ ✤

Rafique hummed softly into the mouthpiece of the phone while waiting on his daughter to answer. Shante picked up the phone and accepted the collect call.

"Hey, baby girl, what's up?"

"Hi, Dad."

"So how was your trip?"

"It was cool. I met all my aunts, uncles, and my granddad. I met Lorraine. She crazy, Dad, I like her. There's something wrong with your father, though."

"Something wrong? What you mean?"

"I think he's really sick."

"What's wrong with him?"

"Well, he looks real bad, and he kept telling me he was a little sick. I guess he don't want me to know how serious it is. But it look serious to me. I think you need to call him."

"Shit, I wanted to talk to you about that letter you sent me. Look, I wrote you about that. You should be getting that letter tomorrow. I'ma call my pop to see what's up. I'ma call you tomorrow and we'll talk about the letter then. You cool?"

"Yeah, I'm cool."

Rafique said goodbye and immediately called his father. After a few rings, Jamil answered. As soon as the recording went off, Rafique spoke, "Abbee, salaam alaikum, what's up?"

"Wa laikum salaam. I'm holding on. I know your daughter has probably told you I haven't been doing so well."

"Yeah, she told me you was kinda sick."

"Yeah, I'm sick. I went to see the doctor last week and he told me after they did some tests that I have cancer."

"What? Cancer? It's from the cigarettes, ain't it?"

"No son, and I use to think if I ever got something like cancer that's what it would be from."

"So what, you gotta get surgery or something?"

"No, son. I got a tumor the size of a golf ball on my liver. They say I got about eight months to live."

A chilling pain shot through Rafique's body that shook his soul. His knees felt weak and his teeth were clinched so tight that his jaw muscles began to ache. At that moment, he pictured in his mind all the times he had with his father and how much time had been wasted.

"Rafique, are you okay?" Jamil interrupted his son's thoughts.

"Yeah, I'm cool."

"Rafique, death is a part of life. We're born into this world and then one day we die. It's what you do while you're here that gives meaning to life. Furthermore, just because the doctors say I only have eight months to live doesn't mean that I do. Allah is the best knower. Pray for me, son, and maybe Allah will grant me a little more time to be here."

Rafique was at a loss for words, and he was in danger of becoming overwhelmed with grief. He fought the grief back, though, by telling his father the news he had. "Abbee, I got some good news."

"Oh, yeah? Well, what is it? Shit, I could use a little good news right now."

"I got a new witness. He told me he was there when Fuzz came up and asked us did we want to go and rob dude. He said I didn't go with him, he left by himself. He gave me his statement today. Now I have to put a brief together under newly-discovered evidence and file a petition to the court. Hopefully, they'll give me a hearing to see if my new evidence is enough to get me a new trial."

"You see, Rafique, I always knew that you would get out of there."

"I ain't out yet, this ain't no guarantee. It's just better than what I had."

Jamil and Rafique talked until Rafique's time on the phone had expired. Rafique hung the phone up and walked slowly back to his cell. He had become very close to his father, and now there was a strong possibility that he would prematurely lose this man who had become a very important person in his life. Rafique passed by Monique, who could see from his body language that something was wrong.

"You okay, Rafique?"

"Yeah. It's just that my father ain't doing so well. I'm cool, though. I got some new evidence earlier today that I feel good about, but right after that I find out my father is dying. So I just went from a high to a low in too short of a time period."

Monique was silent as Rafique spoke. She understood that at that moment he just needed someone to listen to him. So he talked on for a while, relieved that he had the space to get all of these feelings out.

"Thanks, Monique, for just being here to listen, because I really needed to get this shit out. You helped me get some balance back."

"That's the least I could do. Besides, that's what friends are for. It makes me happy when I can help ease your burdens."

Rafique thanked her again and continued on to his cell, where he got in the bed and let sleep help ease his mind.

The following day Rafique met Buff around the notary and they got the statement notarized.

"Look, Buff, I'm going to get copies of this. I'll get you a copy. I got sixty days to get this petition in. I hope this shit works." Rafique then went on explaining the next steps that would be taken. He then shook Buff's hand and thanked him again before departing to go back to their respective blocks.

CHAPTER TWENTY-EIGHT

Thirty days came and went. During this time, Rafique was preparing himself for what the prosecutor would say in response to his petition. He was also stressing because his father wasn't doing too well.

It was a Tuesday afternoon, and Rafique had just stepped out of the law library when he ran into Joe-Joe and Duck. They both had on their brown corduroy coats, and by the look on their faces, Rafique could tell something was up. "What's up y'all?" Rafique wanted to know what was about to happen.

"That nigga Moose on the new-side right now. We getting ready to go over there and pay that nigga a visit," said Joe-Joe as he opened up his coat and showed Rafique his homemade fiberglass knife.

"What's up with you?" Duck asked.

"Man, this thing with my pop is stressing me out."

"He ain't doing to good, huh?"

"Naw, man. Wait for me, I'm going, I got to go get strapped. I'ma be back in like two minutes."

Joe-Joe and Duck looked at one another, but neither said a word. They really didn't want him to go, but they knew no matter what they said it wouldn't stop him from following behind them.

As Rafique rushed to get back off the block, he bumped into Kenyatta.

"Hey, what's up, youngblood? Hoooo, what's up? Man, is everything okay? Rafique had his corduroy coat on. Kenyatta knew that the coat meant trouble.

"Yeah, I'm cool. I just need to take care of something real quick."

Kenyatta was a twenty-year jailhouse veteran. He knew without asking that this was serious business, and his favorite youngin was about to do something that he would most assuredly regret. Kenyatta watched as Rafique hurriedly left the block. He slowly shook his head and hoped that his friend would be okay.

Five minutes later, with his homemade knife tucked in his waistline, Rafique was back in the hallway. On his way to the new-side, anger began to build as he thought of the man who murdered his cousin. All the pain and frustration that he was going through fueled his anger, bringing it boiling to the surface. Rafique was way past the point of no return as all reason and logic fled from the anger that now coursed through his body.

Rafique arrived on the new-side with one thing on his mind. Revenge! Today, Moose would pay. He would not only pay for taking Rafique's cousin's life, but he would pay for everything that went wrong in Rafique's life.

Rafique, Joe-Joe, and Duck had no problem getting on the block where Moose was housed. There was a lot of traffic going to the yard and the three of them just slipped through the crowd. The plan was for Rafique to lure Moose to the back of the block where Joe-Joe and Duck would be waiting. It was a simple plan, and for what they were about to do, simplicity would be the most effective. It all hinged upon Moose not knowing Rafique but Rafique knowing Moose.

As soon as they entered the block, they split up. So far so good. The block was empty since everyone went outside. Rafique hung around up front while Joe-Joe and Duck went to the back. Luckily, Moose wasn't out on the block and he didn't go outside or their hastily put-together plan wouldn't have worked. For the first ten minutes, Moose was nowhere to be seen. Rafique began to get anxious, so he began to question himself. *Yo, what the fuck is you doing? You got too much to lose.*

Suddenly Moose appeared, erasing away all doubts as anger reemerged. Rafique stared hard, waiting for Moose to look his way. Finally, eye contact.

"Damn, old head, what the fuck is you looking at?" Rafique shouted as he slowly approached Moose.

"You got a lot of heart, little nigga, talking to me like that. You know who the fuck I am?"

"Nigga, fuck you, I don't give a fuck about who you supposed to be. Do you know who the fuck I am? As a matter of fact, let's go to the back of the block."

Moose, always in the mood for a physical confrontation, immediately started to the back of the block. Never being very smart, a set-up never crossed his mind.

As soon as Rafique arrived at the back of the block, he turned and waited for Moose with his homemade knife in hand. Moose saw the knife and smiled. Moose was confident since he was nearly twice Rafique's size, so he liked his chances, knife and all. The knife made him focus intently on Rafique. He was totally unaware when Joe-Joe and Duck slipped out of a cell behind him.

"Yo, Moose! Nigga, that was my son you killed!"

Moose turned at the sound of Duck's voice. *What the fuck is Duck talking about?* As this thought breezed through his mind, Moose quickly turned back to face Rafique, but it was too late. Rafique had made his move. While Moose was being distracted for that brief instant, Rafique erased the distance that separated them and began to systematically drive the point of his knife through the brown uniform and flesh.

"Aaaahhh!" Moose let out a yell and threw a wild punch. Rafique ducked and his knife once again parted the muscle and soft flesh of Moose's torso. At the same time, Joe-Joe and Duck jumped on Moose like a pack of ravenous, wild dogs. After being stabbed repeatedly, Moose fell hard to the floor. Once he was down, Duck began to stomp him. Joe-Joe and Rafique looked on for a second, frozen as they watched rage manifested. Joe-Joe snapped out of it first. "Yo, Duck! Come on, man, let's go. Leave him!"

Duck was a man possessed as he ignored Joe-Joe's pleas. He just kept stomping a now motionless Moose. Joe-Joe turned to Rafique. "Get the fuck out of here. I'll get Duck."

Rafique did as his uncle had instructed him. He turned and walked calmly off the block and back to his cell. A half hour later the jail was being locked down. *They must have found Moose.* Rafique immediately started stressing. He was worried about his uncles and whether or not they made it back. He then began to worry about if someone spotted him, and if so, what would happen to the chance that he now had to get out of prison. An internal conflict began to brew, consuming his soul in the process.

Rafique's thoughts then shifted to his father and if things went wrong what would it do to Jamil's fragile state of health. *Damn, why didn't I think of all this shit before?* This thought went unanswered as a piece of mail was dropped into his cell. It was addressed from his father.

"Ain't that a bitch," Rafique said quietly to himself, all thoughts of his own troubles gone as he tore open the envelope.

*IN THE NAME OF ALLAH THE BENEFICENT
THE MERCIFUL*
*"And hold fast to the rope of Allah together and do
not separate."*

My Dear Son,

Inshallah, this letter arrives at a time when all is well with you. I am as well as can be expected. Allah is keeping me and I am in good hands. We talk so much on the phone I'm at a loss for words as to what to say in this letter. I can say this though, I need for you to pray for me. I need for you to make the five prayers for my recovery. But if I am to die soon, I need for you to pray for my soul, that I not touch the hell fire, that I reach instead the paradise Allah has promised in his book, The Holy Quran. Now I pray for you and your eventual freedom. I am with you my beloved son.

Assalamu Alaikum

Love,
Jamil

CHAPTER TWENTY-NINE

Days turned to weeks and weeks to months, and Rafique's name never came up in the Moose incident. Duck wouldn't leave, so he was caught. Joe-Joe, after trying to get Duck to leave, gave up and left him there. Duck stayed behind to take the case, effectively allowing his nephew and brother a chance to get away.

After a few month's had passed, Rafique was approached by Willie Bo-Bo. Willie Bo-Bo lived on the block with him and worked in the laundry room. Once a week he went to the hole to take the brothers who were held there clean sheets and towels.

"Ay, Rafique, I got a note for you from your uncle."

"Thanks Bo-Bo," Rafique replied as he took the note out of Bo-Bo's outstretched hand and proceeded to his cell to read it.

What's up Nephew?

Things don't look too good for me right now. I'm sure that you're aware that Moose is dead. They keep trying to get me to say that somebody was with me, but you know me, I was by myself, why would I lie on another motherfucker. Anyway how's your Pop? I pray that he's making a recovery. He's a real good brother and he deserves better. There are a whole lot of other motherfuckers in this world that deserves that kind of shit. But you know that's just life, the assholes seem to live forever.

Rafique you got a shot man, take advantage of it. Don't sit around all scared of these white folks and let this opportunity slip through your fingers. I got faith in you though and I always knew that you would be the one to make it out of here. I'm out man and this letter has reached its end, so with that I'm letting you know that I'm cool. I love you, and I got this!!!

Assalamu Alaikum,
Duck

A few days after Rafique received the note from Duck, he got a pass for some legal mail. He picked the mail up and took it back to his cell. Rafique's eyes slowly scanned the words of the letter. As his eyes moved further along, his heart rate picked up its pace and his stomach became as unstable as a storm churning the waters of the Atlantic. Rafique had been scheduled for an evidentiary hearing. This is a hearing where you present your new evidence to a judge, and the judge will then determine whether or not it's sufficient enough to warrant a new trial. The hearing was scheduled for ninety days away. Rafique's hands shook and his eyes pooled with tears. This was it. This was what he was praying for, an opportunity to prove his innocence. Rafique dashed out of the cell. He had to let Kenyatta know the good news.

"Ay, Yatt!" Rafique was out of breath as he walked into Kenyatta's cell.

"What's up, youngblood? You alright?"

"I got that hearing, man."

"You got it?"

"Yeah, man."

"Yo, Fique, that's what's up. But you know it ain't over yet. You still got some rumbling to do."

"I know, I know. But it's a step in the right direction. If this shit work out for me and I get out of here, I got you. I ain't gonna be like the rest of these motherfuckers who leave out of these joints and forget about this shit. I ain't never gonna forget this or the dudes I leave behind."

"I know youngblood. Something about you tells me that you ain't like the rest."

"That's something that really bothers me. I mean, how can you walk up and down this motherfucker for years and years with a dude, get as close as a brother to him, and then go home and act as if the relationship never existed? How can you treat somebody you love like that?"

Kenyatta shook his head; he had no answer for Rafique.

"Yatt, man, I swear on everything I love that if I get out of here I'ma do everything in my power to get you the fuck out of here. You don't deserve to be here for the rest of your life. You changed too many lives to not have an opportunity for another shot at life outside these walls."

"Do your peoples know about this?"

"Naw, you're the first person I told."

"Alright, go on and call your family and give them the news."

"Alright, Yatt. I'll be back later on to holla at you."

"Alright, youngblood." Kenyatta's happiness at Rafique's fortune was subdued. It just reminded him of how long he had been imprisoned and how hopeless his situation was. Tears began to leak from his eyes as he watched Rafique leave his cell.

✪ ✪ ✪

Jamil's condition became worse. He was moved from his home to a veteran's hospice. The conditions there were so deplorable that Lorraine was forced to move him back home. Rafique was taking the changes very hard. He couldn't call anymore because during the times he could call, Jamil was heavily medicated.

Things went on like this for a couple months until one day he was called for an unexpected visit. When he arrived in the visiting room, he saw his mother, his daughter, his sisters, and an old friend Stacey. He also saw the jailhouse Reverend. When he saw the reverend conversing with his mother, he knew that his father was gone. At that moment he felt a slow, deliberate, grinding pain. It felt as if his intestines were being pulled through a meat grinder. His knee buckled, causing him to lean against the wall for support. Although Rafique knew that his father was terminally ill and that he would die soon, he still clung to the minute possibility that his father would pull through. Rafique tried to prepare himself for the inevitable, and he thought that he had, but nothing can prepare you for the death of someone you love.

The Reverend approached Rafique, but Rafique walked right by him. Now wasn't the time to talk to a stranger. The Reverend followed Rafique to his seat as he sat down next to his mother. "Rev, I'm cool, I just need to be with my family right now. If I need you later, I'll come talk to you."

The Reverend nodded his head, turned, and walked away.

Tonya looked at her son, tears streaming down her face. "Rafique, Jamil left us."

The words that his mother spoke, brought the pain back in fresh waves and Rafique had no control as the tears once again escaped the prison of his eyes.

"Rafique, we just got back from DC. We were with him and he kept asking for you."

The tears felt hot as they flowed down his face and the pain increased in intensity. Rafique struggled hard to maintain his composure as grief tried to pound him into submission. He was able to hold it together during the time spent with his family, but once back in his cell, he gave in to the hurt as sobs continuously racked his body. Rafique cried as memories of his father paraded through his mind. He cried as the finality of his loss made itself known. He cried until, emotionally exhausted, he fell asleep.

CHAPTER THIRTY

"BZ-9999! You got court!" The ninetieth day was at hand and the C/O's voice shattered the silence and awoke Rafique from his sleep. It was four in the morning and the rest of the block was asleep as Rafique yawned and sat up. Rafique was still very tired, he had a restless night. Sleep was hard to come by because of the anticipation of the day's events. Rafique got up and put on his robe. Silence greeted him as he walked down the empty block to the shower. Twenty minutes later, he was dressed and leaving the cell, heading to the front of the block where he would wait for a guard to escort him to breakfast. After he finished eating, he was taken to the holding cell to change into his suit for court and wait on the sheriffs to pick him up. The sheriffs arrived at quarter to eight and Rafique was handcuffed, shackled, and loaded onto the Blue Goose to take the ride to the new Criminal Justice Center where his hearing was being held.

Damn, I ain't seen a tree in years. Rafique stared in wonderment at things that he used to see every day and paid no attention to. This was another example of things he no longer had access to but he now had an appreciation for. The scenery flew by as he traveled on the highway towards the city. Tired of watching the other cars that passed, Rafique closed his eyes and pictured his upcoming hearing in his mind. Rafique walked through the process step by step. He couldn't see any flaws. *I'm going the fuck home.*

He had arrived. The Criminal Justice Center looked ominous. This building would be the place he received a chance to renew his life. Rafique exhaled. His gut was doing somersaults, and his whole body trembled with anticipation.

The trip to the holding cell went by in a blur. The next thing Rafique knew, they were calling him. It was time. Rafique got up and walked to the front of the cell where he was handcuffed and escorted to the courtroom. Rafique stepped inside and was shocked by the sight that greeted him. The place was jam-packed, full of family and friends. Of course his mother, brother, and sisters were there. Lorraine made the trip, along with all of his family from his father's side of the family. Aisha was there along with his son who sat right next to his big sister. Monique was there and so were all of his aunts, uncles, cousins, and friends. Rafique waved to his supporters and took a seat at the defense table.

"All rise for the Honorable Judge O'Keefe," the bailiff called out, quieting the courtroom.

Everyone stood up as the judge took his seat. The judge peered over his horn-rimmed glasses and pounded his gavel. "This is an evidentiary hearing, are all parties ready?"

"Yes, your Honor," both attorneys responded.

"Okay, let's get the witness in."

The sheriff exited the courtroom. Minutes later he came back in with Buff, who went straight to the witness box. The bailiff approached the stand with a Bible.

"Please rise and state your name."

"My name is Gregory Anderson."

"Could you please place your right hand on the Bible and repeat after me."

After Buff was sworn in, he sat back down and was approached by Rafique's lawyer. Rafique's lawyer cleared his throat.

"Mr. Anderson, could you please tell the court what happened on the night of May 11, 1991."

"Yeah, uh, me, Rafique, Tashi, and Ab was standing on the corner of 52nd and Delancey Street, waiting around, passing time, waiting for the club to open up. At about ten o'clock, Fuzz came up and asked me did I want to go get some money. I said 'What's up?' And he said he wanted to get this dude name Righteous. I said, 'Naw, I'm cool.' Fuzz is a slimy cat and I don't trust him. So he turned to Rafique, Tashi, and Ab and asked them did they want to go, but they all said no. Rafique was real high, he had about ten Valiums. Even if he wanted to go, he wasn't in the condition to do anything."

"Objection, your Honor! Speculation," the D.A. shouted out.

"Sustained. You may continue Mr. Anderson, but just tell us the facts, not your opinion," the judge said, looking down at Buff.

"Anyway, Fuzz left after that. We stood up on the corner until about one or two in the morning before we went to the club."

After Buff finished talking, the D.A. got his chance to cross-examine him. He tried every trick and intimidation tactic he could think of, but none of it worked. Buff remained calm and stuck to the facts. Try as he might, the prosecutor could not get him to waver. Finally, after about an hour the prosecution rested. The judge cleared his throat and his cold blue eyes zeroed in on Rafique. "I'll be back with my decision after this recess. Court will be adjourned until tomorrow morning, nine o'clock." And with the slam of his gavel, he got up and walked to his chambers.

TO BE CONTINUED...

TERREL CARTER

THE TRUTH I TOLD MYSELF

"A Series of Letters From the Men We Are Today, to the Boys We Were Yesterday"

NAACP Youth Committee Graterford Chapter
Box 244, Graterford, PA 19426

"If Only I Knew then What I Know Now"

In effort to correct the wrongs that the following men have done to themselves, their community, their families, and those that may follow in similar paths as they did, a compilation of letters were constructed. These letters are directed to the younger versions of the authors. We discussed ways of effectuating change in order to prevent choices that were detrimental to the lives of ourselves and others. Who knows better to help deter you or help correct you than a wiser version of yourself? Hopefully our youth can identify with these letters and realize that their situations aren't unique These letters seek to change the destructive course some of our youth may be influenced to take in life. Maybe these letters will affect change in their lives, because we can ill afford to lose our sons and with them ourselves again.

TERREL CARTER

Dear Little Dawud,

Yo Cuzz,

I would ask what's good, but I know you going through it right now. I know you feel alone. Reef left for the army. Mal still gone in college. Your mom can't hold a job right now and just living is getting tight around the house. You probably thinking you need to do something right? Something to relieve the pressure off of your mom? That's what men do. Understandable. You're not quite a man yet, though. You are just taking the responsibilities of a man. The things that you feel are your responsibilities are not entirely your burden. It's admirable of you to feel that way though. Because it's not entirely up to you, you don't have to take the drastic steps you're thinking of taking. I could talk about patience but I know being poor is a hurt piece. It messes with you over and over until desperation puts you in a position to act desperately. I won't tell you to wait around for someone to help because there is no one coming. I know you don't have a problem working and you even went and tried to get a couple of jobs but were turned away because you were too young. You have to keep trying. Your pride won't let you work fast food huh? I work in a kitchen for 19¢ an hour now. You gotta push that pride to the side for a minute. Babysteps. Just because you work fast food doesn't mean you have to stay there. You already know an occupation doesn't make you. Drug dealing won't make you, will it? If you don't sell drugs will that make you any less business savvy? Will that determine how much heart you have? Will that make you any less of a hustler? We both know the answer is no. The fact is that you'll hate working fast food so much that you'll work that much harder to get outta there. The life that you about to try to get into, I'm not going to say it's too hard for you because it's not. The consequences don't outweigh the rewards in the long run. That's the main thing. The long run. Not the short term. School is the long term. It has substantial upside. You have upside. You're not stupid. A couple of more years and you are out of school. I know you don't see peer pressure because there is no one asking you to do anything. The fact that they are doing what they are doing with ease and you see yourself more capable than they are is a form of peer pressure that you are applying to yourself. Add that to the fact that you need to pay attention to who your friends are anyway. What they say, how adamant are they about not going to jail? Adamant enough to give you up if it means their freedom. Your loyalty to the wrong people can lead you into a bad situation. Check on some of those dudes history. Especially the older ones. You'll see that they're not as thorough as you think they seemed when you were much younger. Some of those dudes were cowards and will try to use your loyalty to their benefit and your detriment. Hunker down young cuz. Prevention is a form of defense. Defense leads to offense. Hold on a little longer and things will get better….I hope. I can only see the future that impatience holds. It's nothing I'm enjoying.

TERREL CARTER

What's Up Lil Homie,

What's good? How are you doing in school? Your father told me that you are pretty good at baseball. A little bird told me that you want to play for the Phillies when you grow up. I believe you can and when you do, make sure you have some World Series tickets for me! Stick with your dreams. Don't let anyone tell you that you can't play for the Phillies when you get older or anything else you may want to become. I'll be the first to tell you it's going to take some hard work. You're going to have to practice a lot and be dedicated in school. You can't worry about your older friends and what they're doing. They have given up on their dreams. All they want to do is sell drugs and get high. I know it's hard b ecause they're your friends. But selling drugs is going to ruin your life. The fast money, cars, girls, and clothes won't last. If you give up your dreams to sell drugs, your life is going to turn into a nightmare. You'll live with regret of giving up something that you didn't have to. Everything you want right now will be there for you later. You just have to work for it. There's nothing wrong with looking bummy for now. Use it as motivation to become a professional baseball player. Don't use it as an excuse to sell drugs. In the end, you'll be watching the games on TV instead of playing in them. Listen to your father and be a good example for your little brother. He looks up to you. If you sell drugs he'll want to sell them too and you'll ruin his life. Well Lil Homie, that's all for now. Just remember what I said. Be yourself and don't worry what everyone else is doing. In the end, it's your life and you're going to have to live with whatever decisions you make. Make your family proud, but most of all, make yourself proud.

Sincerely,
Marco

Ike,

What's up? I know you're wondering who this is right? It's me or shall I say you in twenty two years. The first thing I want to do is thank you for my current living arrangements. You really looked out for me. I don't have to pay rent and I can play all the sports I want and when I have to go to the bathroom, I don't have to go far because my bathroom is also my bedroom. Oh, and I also have people controlling my every move. Plus you know how I take pride in how I dress? Well I don't have to worry about that either because all I can wear now is brown all day every day. If you haven't figured it out by now we in jail genius, and guess what. We got a life sentence and we been serving it since we was seventeen years old. Man when I think of all the foul things you did it makes me grimace with pain and embarrassment. I say all of the things you did because of the person I am today would never do any of those things that you did back then. But let me slow down for a minute because I know how you hate to be preached to and I am not going to do that period. I am just trying to have a conversation with you about some of the choices you will be making. I know right now you are still like "Yeah, whatever" and I understand that because of the way we were raised. Yeah, pops wasn't there and moms was always working, and that left you and our little brother Chris to fend for yourselves, but I am not buying that as an excuse. Even though mom was at work we still remember the lessons she taught us. We just choose to ignore them. Alright I'm thirty-seven so that would make you about fifteen right? That means you have already picked up your first gun and sold drugs already right? But if I remember right we just got out of Saint Gabriel Hall last year and we have the opportunity to go to West Catholic High to play football but instead we chose to go to De La Salle Vocational with our homies. Bad choices. But all is still not lost because it's still not too late to turn your life around. First you have to man up and realize that you are a leader but you're allowing yourself to be lead by those you claim to lead. I know you are trying to figure out my last statement so I'll give you an example. Do you remember when JoJo stole two dollars from you in the arcade and at first you just laughed it off because JoJo use to be your old head before he started smoking coke. Then everybody in the arcade was like, damn, how you gonna let that smoker still your money" and even though you really didn't care you still pistol whipped JoJo because you didn't want to look weak in front of your squad. If you really were a leader you wouldn't let that peer pressure make you do something that you didn't want to do. So who was really leading who? Do you remember why we said we were getting in a game? Well I do. We said we were trying to take some pressure off our mother. Well guess what? Our mother has terminal bone cancer and the doctor said there's nothing they can do for her. Oh yeah, and our brother had a massive stroke and is living in an adult living home because he can't walk and he has brain damage. Yo, I know that at your age you can't really grasp the magnitude of your decisions and the affect that if will have not only on your life but also on the life of our entire family and friends. And speaking of friends we have one left that we grew up with, the rest of them stop communicating with us once the judge gave us a life sentence. Well at least we didn't mess things up with our family. They still are the only ones we have in our corner after twenty years in prison. But man we really hurt our family. They need us but we can't help them because we are in prison. Look I'm not gonna try and tell you what to do, I'm just giving you a glimpse into what the future holds for us if you keep doing the things that you are doing. I know you have a lot of good in you and that you really want to do right and make our mother proud but right now you lack the courage because you don't want to seem soft or un cool to your homies but trust me being in prison around a bunch of men all day and not being able to be there for our family is more un cool then doing right could ever be. So in closing please think about all the things I said to you in this letter and start really thinking about the decisions you are making and all the people you will hurt if you don't change the ones you are already making.

TERREL CARTER

Big G,

How are you? God willing this message reaches you staying out of trouble and re-thinking your life style. I really didn't know what to say to you taking into consideration how hard headed and dismissive we are at fourteen years old. At that age, we think that we are men and are ready for the world. We never stop to benefit from the wisdom of the people in our lives that have already traveled down the path we are embarking on. I'm talking about those who followed this path personally and those who witnessed the outcome of the lives of people who choose this way. The way or path that I am referring to is the streets or the game, as those in the life call it. Me being someone whom you respect and that you know played that game to the fullest; I hope that you would at least lend me your ear for a minute. After all we were the same person and you would be surprised how identical our life experiences have been. I too came from a broken home and have a real disconnect from my father who really didn't know how to be a father. Sure he was a hard working man, a disciplinarian, and a provider but there is much more to fatherhood. A young man needs someone who shows him real love, that inspires him, that teaches him how to maneuver through the test that face all young men and someone who hasn't lost touch with their younger self. Without these intangible necessities in your upbringing you will seek them elsewhere and often times it's from the wrong people. Just like you, I was exposed to the activities of the streets and I didn't have to go outside of my own household for it. I know that your grandfather is an old hustler who made plenty of money in those streets. Even though he fell back you still witnessed much of his lifestyle before you were even old enough to understand it. That can have psychological impact on you that last a life time. Even he doesn't want you in this game because it caused him so much pain through the years. Don't forget he lost your cousin at the age of nineteen due to that lifestyle. I know you saw your cousin hustling, carrying guns, he and your grandfather feuding over drugs, homicide kicking down the door for him, him getting shot, and much more. His father told me he called you from Gratersford where he is serving a life sentence without parole to talk to you but it doesn't seem to be getting through. Your uncle is serving twenty years in the federal prison system and your mother tells me he tries to talk to you also but to no avail. Speaking of your mother, she has expressed to me that she regrets you having to see her go through the struggles with drug addiction and feels responsible for your behavior. I'm here to tell you that despite what you seen from her, she has done and is doing all she can to steer you away from that lifestyle but you seem to be too far into it now. Despite all of the things that we have been expose to I'm here to tell you that in the end we always have a choice to go right and it's up to us to make that choice. Believe me before your life in the game plays out you will have more than one opportunity and reason to do something legitimate. Learn how to start a business, choose a legitimate product, or service and hustle legitimately. Don't fall for the myth that the game will dumb you up to believe that there is more money in it then in legitimate goods, services and industries which is very far from the truth. You can have all the things that you seek without the consequences of the game. Instead of making your mother cry you can make her proud. You may feel that being a criminal is natural because of what you have been exposed to but something as inherently destructive, violent and parasitic could never be natural. You will lose close friends to that lifestyle and you will find out through adversity that people you thought to be friends weren't. In the end all you will have on this earth is your family if you're fortunate. Normally you end up with the same woman you constantly ignored in your corner, your mother. Stay in control of your life while you still can because it can be snatched away from you in a blink of an eye. I love and have an invested interest in you getting it together. If you get it right we will both be successful. I'll write again soon and until then, take care of yourself.

Love Always
You

GUILTY REFLECTIONS - REVISED EDITION

THE TRUTH I TOLD MYSELF

To order the free, complete booklet of "The Truth I Told Myself," please write to NAACP Youth Committee, Graterford Branch, P.O. Box 244, Graterford, PA 19426. Please include the number of booklets you would like.

ORDER FORM

iDream Publications
P.O. Box 28910
Philadelphia, PA 19151

Name:_____

SBI #:_____(if applicable)

Address:_____

City/State: _____

Zip Code: _____

Guilty Reflections Revised Edition Quantity:_____

Guilty Reflections II Quantity:_____

Cost: $15.00 + shipping & handling of $4.95
Add $1.00 to postage for each additional purchase
Shipping & handling to prisons…..FREE

Please make money orders and
institutional checks payable to:
iDream Publications

Allow five to seven business days for delivery.
Thank You.

CPSIA information can be obtained
at www.ICGtesting.com
Printed in the USA
BVHW040147230422
635156BV00002B/2